T0169527

The
Survival
League

The Survival League

Gordan Nuhanović

translated by
Julienne Eden Bušić

OOLIGAN
PRESS

The Survival League
© 2005 Gordan Nuhanović

All rights reserved. No part of this book may be reproduced or transmitted in any form or by any means, electronic or mechanical, including photocopying, recording, or by any information storage and retrieval system, without permission in writing from the publisher.

Second Printing
ISBN13: 978-1-932010-06-0

This publication is the product of Ooligan Press and the Publishing Program at Portland State University. It was produced entirely by the students of this program. For credits, see back matter.

Publication of this work is partially underwritten by a grant from the Ministry of Culture of the Republic of Croatia.

The stories in this collection were originally published in Croatian by the Croatian publishing house, Antun Gustav Matos. English translations and author photo by Julienne Eden Bušić.

Slightly different English versions of "Something about Daisies," "How I Transcended Trichinosis," and "The First and Last Punker" have appeared in *The Gobshite Quarterly*. Likewise, "The Barefoot Experience" appeared in *Konch*.

Ooligan Press
Department of English
Portland State University
PO Box 751
Portland, OR 97207-0751
503.725.9748
ooligan@ooliganpress.pdx.edu
www.ooliganpress.pdx.edu

This book is set in Adobe Caslon Pro
and printed in the United States of America.

My deep appreciation to everyone who contributed to the English publication of my book, with special thanks to Julie and the Ooligan Press team.

G.N.

Contents

Introduction to Croatia

Some might find it difficult to locate Croatia on the map due to its modest size and configuration. The country is approximately the size of the state of West Virginia, covering 56,542 square kilometers of land (about 20,355 square miles) and 35,000 square kilometers of sea (about 12,600 square miles). Croatia stretches from the Alps in the northwest to the Pannonian lowlands and the banks of the Danube River in the east. In its center is the vast Dinaric mountain range; in the south, it extends to the coast of the Adriatic Sea and its many islands. The Croatian coastline is 5,835 kilometers long (close to 4,000 miles), 80 percent of which comprises islands, cliffs, and reefs. Of more than a thousand islands, 50 of them inhabited, the largest are Krk and Cres.

Croatia is a Central-European as well as a Mediterranean country. It boasts verdant plains and valleys, warm seas and snow-covered mountains, farmers and fishermen, bustling towns and endless undisturbed beaches. Only several hundred kilometers away from major European cities such as Vienna, Budapest, and Venice, Croatia offers great diversity within its borders. The majority of today's population (about four and a half million) is Croatian; national minorities include Serbs, Slovenes, Hungarians, Bosnians, Italians, Czechs, Germans, and Ruthenians. Approximately 800,000 people live in Zagreb, the capital of Croatia and its major cultural, financial, and academic center. The main religion is Roman Catholic.

The area known as Croatia in modern times has been inhabited since the Stone Age, long before the Croats moved into the region. During the Paleolithic era, Neanderthals lived in the northwestern region near Krapina. Early in the 20th century, the skeletal remains of "Krapina Man" were found in nearby caves, along with stone tools such as scrapers.

In recorded history, it is known that the area was colonized by both the Celts and the ancient Greeks, who established a colony on the island of Vis in the 4th century B.C. during their explorations of the Adriatic. The ancestors of Croatia's current Slav population settled in parts of the Roman provinces of Pannonia and Dalmatia in the 7th century and accepted Christianity in the 9th century.

The first King of Croatia, Tomislav of the Trpimirović dynasty, was crowned in 925. Tomislav, *rex Chroatorum*, united the Dalmatian and Pannonian duchies and created a powerful state. The medieval Kingdom of Croatia reached its peak during the reign of King Petar Krešimir IV (1058–1074). Soon thereafter, internal strife led to the loss of the kingdom's independence.

In 1102 a "personal union" between Hungary and Croatia was established under the auspices of the Hungarian monarch. Although Croatia remained linked with Hungary for eight centuries, the Croats were allowed to choose their rulers independently of Budapest. Croatia retained its own governing Diet and was headed by a Ban, or Viceroy.

After 1526 most of Croatia came under Turkish rule. In 1527, the Croatian feudal lords accepted Hapsburg rule in exchange for a common defense and the safeguarding of their privileges. During the following century, Croatia served the Hapsburg Empire as an outpost in the defense of Central Europe from a Turkish onslaught.

The power of the Croatian nobility was increasingly weakened by the centralization and "Germanization" of the Hapsburgs, which led to a resurgence of national consciousness among the Croats. In 1848, Hungary subjected Croatians to "Magyarization"—forced assimilation to the language and culture of the Magyars, or ethnic Hungarians—and imposed a system of legislation that endangered Croatian autonomy within the Hapsburg Empire. Joseph Jelačić Ban of Croatia, had the Diet pass its own revolutionary laws, including the abolition of serfdom. Jelačić's forces also marched against the Hungarian revolutionaries in the 1848–1849 uprisings in the Hapsburg Empire. A dual Austro-Hungarian monarchy was established in 1867; Croatia proper and Slavonia were included in the Kingdom of Hungary, and Dalmatia and Istria in the Austrian empire. The following year Croatia, united with Slavonia, became an autonomous Hungarian crownland governed by a Ban responsible to the Croatian Diet.

Despite the achievement of autonomy in local affairs, Croatia remained restless because of continuing Magyarization and Germanization. Cultural and political Croat and South Slav organizations arose, notably the Croatian Peasant Party, founded in the early 20th century. With the collapse of Austria-Hungary in 1918, the Kingdom of Serbs, Croats, and Slovenes (later renamed Yugoslavia) was formed, although the Croatian Parliament never ratified the Act of Unification. Serbs dominated the new state and promoted centralization, ignoring Croat desires for a federal structure.

On the eve of the Second World War, the Croatian nation found itself divided politically. The majority of the population supported the peaceful Peasant Party, whose leader, Stjepan Radić, had been assassinated in the Parliament in Belgrade in 1928. Two extremist parties, the right-wing Ustashis and the Communists, offered alternatives. The Axis occupation of Yugoslavia in 1941 allowed the Croatian radical right to come into power, leading to brutal excesses in dealings with political opponents (as was the case in other European countries under control of the Axis-allied governments, such as France and Italy). An anti-fascist partisan movement emerged early in 1941 under the command of the Communist Party, led by Josip Broz Tito. Croatia became part of Yugoslavia in 1945, under Tito's leadership. The end of the war brought more brutalities and violence, this time perpetrated by Tito's forces.

Repressive trends after Tito assumed power led ultimately to the "Croatian Spring" of 1970–1971, when intellectuals and students in Zagreb organized demonstrations for greater civil liberties and Croatian autonomy. The regime violently suppressed the protest and imprisoned the leaders.

In 1980, after Tito's death, political, ethnic, social, and economic difficulties multiplied, and the federal government began to disintegrate. Croatian demands for secession increased. The emergence of Slobodan Milošević in Serbia and other related events provoked an adverse reaction in Croatia, followed by a rise in support for independence.

The year 1991 was a new beginning for Croatia: the Croatian Parliament declared independence from Yugoslavia, after which the Yugoslav National Army (JNA) attempted to maintain the status quo by force of arms. Many Croatian cities, notably Vukovar and the UNESCO-protected "Pearl of the Adriatic," Dubrovnik, came under attack by the army and Serbian paramilitary forces. The Croatian Parliament severed all remaining ties with Yugoslavia in October of that year.

The civilian population fled the areas of armed conflict en masse. Entire towns and cities were leveled, cultural monuments were destroyed, and approximately ten thousand people were killed, the majority of them civilians. The aggression displaced hundreds of thousands of people, many of whom were given refuge in the Republic of Croatia outside of combat zones—in Croatian tourist hotels, church properties, and so on.

The border city of Vukovar underwent a three-month siege, during which most of the city buildings were destroyed and the population was forced to flee. The city fell to Serbian paramilitary forces in late November 1991. Several United Nations-sponsored cease-fires followed, until the Yugoslav National Army retreated from Croatia into Bosnia and Herzegovina, its next target.

Soon after the collapse of Vukovar, official recognition of Croatia's independence began. By the end of January 1992, most of the world had recognized Croatia as a sovereign state.

Armed conflict in Croatia remained sporadic and mostly on a small scale until 1995. In early August, working in close cooperation with United States advisors, Croatia started "Operation Storm" and quickly regained control of its occupied territories, almost one third of the country in the areas bordering Serbia and Bosnia–Herzegovina. A few months later, the war ended with the signing of the Dayton Agreement.

Croatia's first democratically elected president, Franjo Tudjman, a former Partisan general, came to power in a landslide victory in May 1990. President Tudjman died in late 1999, and new elections took place. Succeeding President Tudjman was Stipe Mesić, who was given a second mandate in January 2005.

The wounds of war have begun to heal in Croatia, and economic recovery and reform are under way. Croatia has become a member of the United Nations and the Council of Europe as well as several other important regional and international organizations. It is currently in the process of joining the European Union and lobbying for NATO membership.

The arts have also sprung to life. The leading scientific and cultural institute, the Croatian Academy of Arts and Sciences (HAZU) founded in 1861, comprises nine programs and various science entities, museums, galleries, and institutes. Croatia boasts four universities, located in Zagreb, Rijeka, Split, and Osijek, as well as 26 state institutes and 500 libraries. Every year a wealth of cultural and artistic festivals take place around the country, including the Music Biennial in Zagreb, the Croatian Film Festivals in Pula and Motuvun, the International Children's Festival in Šibenik, and the Folklore Show in Zagreb.

Today Croatia has several professional and amateur theater companies and a thriving literary scene. Each year new Croatian authors make their mark outside the Republic of Croatia. Gordan Nuhanović is one of the many talented Croatian writers who will soon have the worldwide audience they deserve.

The First and Last Punker

In the early 1980s, the punk rock scene was very strong in my hometown. If you asked a kid on the street what he wanted to be when he grew up, he'd answer arrogantly and without hesitation: a rock star! An unbelievable number of bands appropriated all the available residential spaces (cellars, bicycle shops, areas intended for hanging out laundry to dry), but there were very few places to hang out at night. Besides, the café owners nurtured a pathological intolerance toward punkers. The continental climate, with its cold evenings, drove the punkers to risk entering cafés where their presence was unwelcome.

G.N. ✚

The First and Last Punker

Exactly at noon, I started working the first shift of my life.

"The coffee machine always has to be clean and plugged in," my boss, Bato, warned me. Old Gaggia,* as it was called, was to be turned off at 10 PM, even if bullets were flying outside. This was a direct quote from Bato: "The machine doesn't get turned on for anyone once it's turned off, is that clear?"

I drank in Bato's every word. "And if someone has a complaint about it," he said in a raised tone so that everyone still in the café could hear, once and for all—they could just come to *him*, Bato Vozetic.

"And one more thing," he remembered, lowering his voice. "If a punker comes in, you serve him whatever drink he orders, but call me on the phone immediately. Is that clear?"

"Sure, Bato," I answered, after which Bato lit his cigarette with great gusto, using the Zippo lighter on which was written *US Army*. It worked during hurricanes and under water, and would spark up even if it was out of lighter fluid, because Bato's Zippo US Army lighter had a false bottom with a secret tank.

"That's it," he concluded as he chugged down his Ballbuster— actually, two shots in one. I held the metal tray just the way Bato had taught me, from the bottom, resting it on the tips of all five fingers of my left hand. I placed a cloth over the clean ashtrays, and by the time you could say *boo* I was strutting among the booths taking my first orders. I felt Bato's eyes on my back. What he wanted was a

---

*   *Gaggia is the name of an Italian company that makes fancy espresso machines.*

waiter as dependable as his US Army Zippo lighter—a waiter who would notify him posthaste at the first sight of a punker. He gave me three percent of the day's earnings, an extra hand from 7 PM on, two free drinks during my shift, and the key to the jukebox.

"So," he asked me as he was leaving, "you remember what I told you?"

A lot of stuff was filtering through my head at that moment.

"Punkers," he repeated. "My number's on the coffee machine."

Oh, yeah, that, of course. I gave him a high five as he left the bar. He could depend on me to make that call.

My first punker contaminated the café by coming in goose-stepping, wearing those big black clodhoppers. I could feel the shift in the air for almost a full minute after he settled into a booth in the back, crossed one leg over his knee, and lit a cigarette with one of those disgusting plastic lighters that are always plugging up.

I was dumbfounded for a moment, shifting around within my territory behind the counter. And then I realized my hands were hanging listlessly at my thighs, which was inappropriate; a waiter's hands must always be occupied, even if the bar is empty. There are glasses in the sink to be washed. Or dirty ashtrays, or else the terrace is a mess. There's always something. A waiter's idle hands attract trouble. That wasn't just Bato's opinion; everyone who had the habit of kicking back against the coffee machine felt the same way.

"A double coffee," requested my first punker, adding: "And a glass of regular water."

I emptied the machine of the previous dregs and filled it with freshly ground coffee, pulled the handle, and pressed the "on" button: imagine a tired cat lounging in the sun. Just listen to the sound of the Gaggia, and you get the audio version of a kitty siesta on a long-forgotten summer morning in some small border town.

As a thin stream of coffee slowly filled the punker's cup, a chorus of "God Save the Queen" boomed from the jukebox, a song I had selected myself, along with several others, maybe because of the punker in the booth. And I hadn't forgotten his glass of water. With one cube of ice. I approached him in the designated manner, from the right side.

"Here you are," I said graciously, but the punker was obnoxiously clunking his dirty shitkickers to the rhythm of "God Save the Queen."

Later, after having served punkers in similar situations, I would take pleasure in delaying that phone call. I'd tidy up the buffet, replace the ashtrays, or, believe it or not, play a hand of picado. And the time would pass slowly in an endless procession of minutes rising out of the malicious steam of the Gaggia. But then all of a sudden I'd be overcome by panic. It always seemed that I had put it off too long, so in a feverish rush I'd dial Bato's number. Of course it didn't take me long to learn it by heart; even now, even though Bato has given up his lease, I could recite the number in my sleep. Although he's probably changed it by now, or at least has an additional number between the first two. But as a final option I could always call information and ask for Bato Vozetic's number, address: Way of the Cross Street; suburb: "Croatian Victims," on the other side of the tracks.

Bato threw out my first punker more gently than he did the others, probably so as not to discourage me right at the beginning. He didn't even cuff him, he just grabbed him by the collar of his leather jacket and yanked him along the stairs toward a little piece of clear sky. With his free hand he maintained balance as they slid along the tiles, slick with condensed steam from the Gaggia. The part of the job I got three percent for I took care of right away and in the proper manner: first, I rinsed out the punker's undrunk cup of coffee, then replaced his ashtray, and most important, smoothed out the seat fabric his punker butt had defiled during the last half hour. As I sauntered over to the booth, there was no sign whatsoever that a punker had been there just moments before. Nothing but a thin stripe of smoke suspended around the halogen light.

Bato ejected the punkers in a lackadaisical manner. Frontal assault to the liver, but a blunt blow, as though he were performing some stultifyingly boring activity which had long ago lost its attraction. Bato's face resembled a mother's breast. Without a hint of anger. It was a weird kind of calm in light of the actions that were to follow, and sometimes it even seemed as though he were going to rest his head on the punker's shoulder. Bato Vozetic's fist usually gyrated in the air for a moment before centering in to the smallest centimeter on the punker's nose, usually from the left, since Bato was a righthander. As the punker writhed around on the floor, Bato would raise his leg back in an expression of disgust and go for his kidneys. But the punkers were always coming back to the café. The one knocked out the night before would show up again the next morning, with spots of dried blood on his lips, naturally. Their orders never changed—a double coffee and a glass of ordinary water.

"With ice, if ya got it."

"Sure, one or two cubes?"

Their throats must be dry as hell, I figured as I plunked in the two cubes.

Bato rented from one guy, Labud, who sublet from another guy who never came around, which made things a little murky: consider what to do if all of a sudden the real owner, who was never around, was standing at the bar. Who would you serve first? Some would blurt out immediately: the real owner first! But wait just a minute! Isn't Bato the one who's paying me three percent of the daily profits? I was sure of one thing, though: The guy Bato rented from, Labud, the one who sublet from the guy who never came around, he was the one who got served last. The end.

You wouldn't think so, but the punker population is fairly small, the old ones disappear and there are fewer and fewer young ones to fill the empty space. So since Bato was always throwing out the same punkers, he started having doubts about himself, his skills. Always the same facial bones, the same system of defense. He felt like he was losing his confidence, and when I'd report the appearance of a punker in the place, it would take him longer and longer to intervene, even though they still got on his last nerve.

His lease with Labud was running out soon.

"Hello, Vozetic residence," said Bato's wife.

"I'm the waiter, I need Bato, it's an emergency."

"Just a moment," she answered in a pleasant tone.

"Hello, this is Bato."

I told him: "I've got a punker here!"

"What does he look like?" He wanted me to describe him.

"Listen," he said after hearing my description of the punker in the booth: "That's my son!"

It was like the phone wires were crackling.

"He went punk not long ago," he added. "But that doesn't matter. I'll be right there."

And then he showed up. Approached the counter, ordered a Ballbuster, first a double, two in one, and then a repeat.

"From tomorrow on, Labud's your boss," he said.

I asked him what was going to happen to him.

He was going back to work for the forest service: pulling corpses out of the woods, that's what he'd done his entire life, he enjoyed it, it relaxed him. No punkers, just him, Bato Vozetic, and the forest.

He placed his palms on the counter. If one were to judge by his powerful hands, crisscrossed by a vigorous web of blue veins, then one would say it was the Croatian Forest Association's lucky day!

He paid for his Ballbusters and lumbered over to throw out his last punker. I knew he wasn't performing some historical act here, just a routine job he felt compelled to do until his lease ran out.

No matter how exhausted they are after last call, totally alone and confronted with the emptiness of the café, waiters are always thinking about their phlebitis and their spines, which are under constant pressure from the unnatural posture leaning over the counter. They spill their guts to the coffee machine because, among all the disinterested inventory, only it seems to have a soul.

"So, old Gaggia," I said, "you know I had only the best of intentions."

Actually, coffee machines sort of stutter at times and it takes them a while to spit out what they have to say.

That's when the shadows of ousted punkers start to glide along the booths, chains clanking, the heavy buckles on their jackets flashing threateningly in the direction of my barren tabernacle.

"At one point in their careers," old Gaggia confessed, "there was a real danger that waiters would start holding conversations with their coffee machines."

Something about Daisies

I was always intrigued by what drove a man to feverishly mow down his own lawn. Is it a subconscious desire for perfect proportions or an expression of deep antagonism toward untamed Nature? Hard to say. At any rate, I began working on several versions of this story to the sound of an electric lawnmower in the neighborhood. When I came to a certain point, I would be at a loss to explain that obsession. Should I send the main characters to the loony bin and punish them by continually playing MC5's "Kick Out the Jams"? Maybe. And then in the newspapers I saw an advertisement for "English Lawns." The company guaranteed a "perpetual green carpet, just like on the postcards for Hyde Park and Windsor." The ad hit the bull's-eye of the Croatian dream. This was the only time I regretted having no talent for business.

G.N. ✚

Something about Daisies

English lawns were popular then. A company even specialized in that type of grass. They delivered it right to the home—that is, to the garden. Two to three days before the lawn was spread, they would prepare the soil. The workers were orderly and clean. They didn't try to sponge beers and didn't leave cigarette butts on the veranda as they worked quietly and—more importantly—industriously, and their work uniforms, which were the nuanced green of young grass, looked surprisingly natty. Beba enjoyed watching them work as she stood on her veranda.

Afterward they took a roller and flattened out the plot of earth. A strong May sun broke out the day the grass was to be laid. Right in front of Beba's eyes, the workers unrolled the English lawn as though it were a big carpet, smoothed out the corners and edges, and stretched it out from all sides to remove any undesirable hillocks. They sprinkled some areas with black loam taken from special bags. Then they uncoiled a hose and gave the lawn a good, long watering with that characteristic spray whose mist shimmers in the air like golden sawdust.

Beba gladly accepted the advice of one of the workers, a certain Marjanovic, if she recalled correctly, who said it was better not to tread on the English lawn. If absolutely necessary, however, then it should be with slippers of impregnated rubber from their own special line of products.

Of course Beba agreed. She would keep two pairs on the veranda at all times. She and her husband lived alone, she said, and thus did not have to worry about children ruining the lawn. They had gotten rid of their dog long ago.

"What about cats?" asked the lanky worker. "Will they be a problem?"

"I have an air gun. Well, actually, my husband does," Beba admitted with a wry smile, "for the worst cases." The worker, an unexpectedly distinguished and sympathetic gentleman, perhaps a bit thin (though this was the way Beba liked them), thanked her, wished her and her English lawn the very best, and left as ceremoniously as he had come.

Returning from work, Beba's husband Franjo found her rapturously gazing upon the English lawn from the raised veranda. Under her arm she held a handful of free advertisements from the company, which meant that she had stood there for who knows how long, relishing the new lawn.

"The color!" Beba said without raising her head. "Just look at the color!" And as a matter of fact, the deep green was especially enchanting. Beba's husband, Franjo, hooked his arm around her waist and gently patted the little roll of fat under her apron several times, to let her know he thoroughly shared her enthusiasm.

It was early on a windless afternoon, and the blades of grass fluttered like filaments on a carpet. But if you got close, really close, as though you were about to step onto the green surface, you could feel the submissiveness of these green blades, as if this were not some ordinary grass a child would roll around on or spit or pee on or grab handfuls of. You could say without hesitation that this grass was special, and that it had come into existence as the result of the fusion of the best grasses in the world in laboratories where one would never be confronted with plain old grass—or God forbid, a soiled plot of turf—in an atmosphere of sterilized ampules, white gloves, and spindly, elongated test tubes, and under a glass that enlarges everything a thousand times over. This was the magical process that results ultimately in the desired deep green color, the softness of the blade, and the unique appearance that has delighted the eye for generations.

All this went through Beba's mind that evening as she watered the lawn, guided by the reflector she had pointed in the required direction. Moving slowly in her special slippers of impregnated rubber, Beba sensed a softness and harmony under her soles, and waves of pleasure pulsed through her body, as though she were delighting in the ministrations bestowed in the best of massage salons.

She fell asleep for the first time in many years with her head turned toward her husband.

The next morning, she hustled immediately out to the veranda, into a blinding late spring sun that shimmered up from the green surface. At first she thought she was being deceived by a tricky play of light. She squinted, as her sunglasses were not within reach, then shadowed her eyes with the palm of her hand as best she could. But there could be no doubt: the English lawn was inundated with daisies, their pale yellow buds quivering from one end of the lawn to the other, grouped more densely in some spots, probably where an excess of water had stood.

She put on her slippers and walked onto the lawn.

She yanked the daisies out by their roots. Some were stubborn. She cut her finger on one of the stalks, and a deep red bead of blood appeared on her fingertip. Amazingly, Beba would overlook a daisy here and there; then she would have to retrace her steps. She plucked them out for about half an hour, until she was winded. Her footprints left indentations on the lawn. Of course, the worker had told her it was not recommended to stand for extended periods on the lawn; at the most, for twenty-five minutes, even in the super slippers. So she tiptoed immediately onto the concrete walkway. Sweat had broken out under the armpits of her bathrobe; something itched, but there was no rash. She felt a sting in the front part of her heart, and an acid heartburn rose up in her gullet. She had all the early symptoms of the flu.

Beba returned to the veranda, shaken. She hadn't noticed that she was still holding the bundles of daisy roots in both hands. In confusion, she threw them into the garbage can. Down below in the yard, the pale yellow buds continued to erupt into the sunlight.

Beba kept to the instructions. Watering twice daily, early in the morning and late at night. Raking during the day with a special jointed rake. Spreading humus once during the week as recommended—two or three handfuls, no more.

But by lunchtime, daisies had again popped up all over the lawn. *Unbelievable!* Beba thought. *Just like in a village meadow!*

She had bags under her eyes, blue capillaries veining her face, and a group of wrinkles above her eyebrows—several deep and crosswise, and two diagonals that came together at the end of her nose bone. Beba was at the age where she needed to avoid stress. Long coffee klatsches on the veranda—that was how Beba imagined the few years left to her and her husband.

They got along well. Their foreign currency account promised them a secure old age. Franjo still worked, but only part-time, as adviser to the director of a local bank, more for himself than for the money. They were set, so to speak, and now they ought to enjoy themselves, satisfy their needs, and that meant just that. They should be able to have a coffee on the veranda and feast their eyes on the English lawn. *Is that asking too much?* Beba asked herself as she looked at the daisies.

There must be some seedbed in the neighborhood, Beba concluded. In the days that followed, she had a two-meter-high wall built, a snow-white wall not only to prevent the spread of the daisies, but also to serve as a contrast to the English green. Her husband was against it, against walls in general, but he wanted his wife to be happy. Actually, what he wanted was a little peace and quiet, nothing more. This they had, until the next morning. The lawn was again inundated with daisies, from edge to edge, as though someone had gone out and planted them under cover of darkness.

Beba watered the lawn, as she did every morning, but a bit absently, not really paying attention to where or how long she trod on the lawn, the hose twisted between her legs like a subjugated snake.

She needed to act quickly and decisively.

Everyone on the street had heard about Beba's problem. Her neighbor had mentioned to her in passing, over the fence, that there was a machine you could buy to pull out daisies. At first this sounded insane to Beba: *a machine that got rid of daisies! How could that be possible?* But she began to mull the idea over.

One day, when the daisies had almost overtaken the entire lawn, Beba again asked her neighbor at the end of the road about the machine, just in passing, as though she didn't really care, more as though it were just an object of curiosity. He, holding a shovel in his hand, could only repeat what he himself had heard: it was a machine that pulled out daisies and left the grass untouched. Supposedly it could be purchased in Hungary, in special shops. The neighbor shrugged his shoulders. He didn't know any more about it, except that a lot of people had similar problems.

Beba thought long and hard, taking everything into account. She didn't want to get carried away or to become a source of amusement for her neighbors. *What kind of machine could this be? Maybe something like a vacuum cleaner? That's ridiculous,* she thought; *that makes no sense at all. Maybe, say, it was a smart, highly sensitive machine programmed to distinguish between the stalks of the daisies and the grass. Depending on the width of the specimen? That could actually explain it!*

That morning, Beba plucked out as many of the daisies as possible, considering her spine was already pinched from the daily bending over and straining. Besides, since she was allowed to tread on the grass no longer than twenty or twenty-five minutes so as not to damage it, she was limited as to how much she could accomplish. At any rate, she waited for her husband to come home from work, secretly tossed her passport into her purse, mumbled something halfway intelligible to him—she was going to the graveyard or something—got into the car, and headed off toward the Hungarian border town of Szegedtvaroszi, to the Agrometro store where she figured she could find these machines.

This crazy Hungarian language! She used her hands and legs to explain what she was looking for. The manager of the firm even came out. Beba finally took him outside, into the store's garden area. He was a mistrustful type, especially curt to uppity foreigners. At least that's how he looked at her, as though he saw a hundred imperfections in her appearance. All the while, he sent furtive eye signals to two other salespeople in the corner.

Since there were no daisies in the garden, Beba squatted above the tulips, looking the manager in the eye, and began pulling the tulips out by their roots, just as she did the daisies on her lawn. The manager scowled with his single row of bushy eyebrows. She noticed that he had hair in his nostrils. She continued to pluck the tulips, the Paris blues, the Swiss yellows, the Hungarian greens, the Brazilian oranges, until the manager indicated with an abrupt movement that he would no longer allow the desecration of the

Agrometro lawn. The two salespersons came forward with clenched fists and grabbed Beba to remove her from the garden. As they pulled and shoved her toward the main office, she ripped her pantyhose and broke a heel. A blossom from her hat fell onto the head manager's shoe, and he brushed it off furiously.

She was given a fine. It was a large number of forinths, so many that Beba was forced to exchange all the German marks she had secretly taken from her household savings. When she started the car to head home, it was in reverse, and she gave a substantial bump to the car parked behind her. Mud was caked under her long nails, her hair was sticking out in all directions, and she quietly cursed as she sped into the first curve of the road. She could hardly wait to get home and into the tub.

It started to sprinkle at the border. A big cloud bank hovered overhead. The windshield wipers barely worked, and she couldn't see a thing. Everything was gray and fuzzy. She had to pull over to the side of the road and wait until it cleared up. She noticed that the hem of her skirt was wet. The car was leaking somewhere, this expensive car they had bought in Germany, with an automatic transmission and the power to reach the speed of 100 kilometers in just 4.3 seconds. She felt like weeping out of sheer frustration, but fear suddenly overcame her. She was alone on the road. It was pouring down rain. She started the car. "Whatever happens, happens," she whispered to herself.

She arrived home after midnight. A light was burning in the kitchen. Before she opened the door, she tidied her hair, wiped the smeared makeup from around her eyes, and scraped the mud from her heels. *Hmm, the heel really did break after all,* she confirmed as she unlocked the front door. Franjo was sitting at the table with an empty glass in his hand, looking like someone who had come to terms with Fate during the previous few hours. He nodded to her and transferred the glass to his other hand. He was silent, completely silent. The television was turned off, which was contrary to Franjo's habits.

Beba hung up her coat. Then it occurred to her that she hadn't prepared an explanation for her long absence. She stopped in her tracks in the middle of the kitchen. No one said a word. When she finally opened her mouth to speak, Franjo held up his hand.

"Don't say a thing, it's OK," he said.

"What do you mean?" Beba asked, as her facial expression softened.

"What? I said everything was fine." Franjo's voice had the depth of a preacher's in an acoustic church.

"All these years," he began as he stroked his glass, "I've wanted to tell you. And now I think is the time."

Beba situated herself on the edge of a chair, her head tilted toward him in order to hear better. She felt a rivulet of makeup trickling down her cheek, and her buttocks felt slick from the humidity she had brought in from outside, chafing her.

"I've always been inactive," Franjo began, as though he were drawing on a special form of wisdom as ancient as the Bible. "You know what I'm talking about."

"I have no idea," Beba replied. She allowed herself a little smile. "What are you blathering on about? Have you been drinking? It's late, and you work tomorrow."

"You know," he said, "it happens to everyone, this stroke of natural bad luck, or whatever, that deprives you of what you deserve, and it's not a rare occurrence, I'm telling you, Beba, no matter what you think. But anyhow, it's your natural right, and I can't blame you." Then he stopped and eyed her closely.

Beba turned on the faucet. Some inner flame was licking at her throat. Despite his grim expression, Franjo's face had the purity of a child's—at least that's how it appeared to her, illuminated in the kitchen light. He stopped for a moment, expecting her to turn off the water. Then he began again to speak.

"You can't blame me for it. I tried everything. You, my dear, don't know anything about it, because I didn't want to burden you, and I had my stupid male pride, or whatever you want to call it, and it was strong enough to prevent me from being honest with you. I lied to you so many times about going on business trips when I was really taking various treatments, one by one, in all the best clinics. I tried Viagra, various handmade balms—where do you think my ulcer came from? And these medicines I'm always taking, they've prescribed a million of them. They even prescribed hookers. But, honeybun, I'm sooooo sorrrrrry, even the hookers didn't help: I just couldn't get it up!"

Silence again descended.

Beba, absorbed in thought, squinted down at the white floor tiles as Franjo continued.

"I wanted to tell you, Beba, that whoever he is, you have my full understanding." Franjo's words were drowned out by the squeaking of the chair on the floor tiles as he raised his limp body from it, touching as he did the light hanging from the ceiling with his graying head. It moved, left–right, elongating their shadows for a moment, as at the end of a movie.

"Oooooh—" That was all Beba could say as Franjo disappeared into the darkness of the bedroom. "Ooooooh!"

She felt her legs shaking, and a sudden weakness overwhelmed her, so she was forced to prop herself up on the radiator, next to the window. She looked outside. The rain was letting up, and the reflector threw a dim, directed light upon the English lawn. It was a 500-watt reflector from which no daisy could escape.

As she looked out on the English lawn, her bright red lips uttered these few words, softly, as though she were taking a sacred oath: *Tomorrow I'm going to pave it over.*

How I Transcended Trichinosis

Some of my stories are motivated by the culture of nutrition in our Balkan outpost. Pork is a basic food item, probably the most important link in the food chain, just as beef is to Texas, or the seal to the polar regions. Thus the spread of trichinosis among the pig population in recent years has had a traumatic effect on many residents, dividing them into the "for" or the "against." I experienced one such shocking scene in my hairdresser's salon, and then rewrote and transformed it into fiction. The story was first published in the Christmas section of a Croatian daily newspaper.

G.N. ✚

Trichinosis /trik-i-'nōs-is/ n. latin. trichinosis, Serbian. trihinoza, German. Trichinose; a condition caused by worm-shaped parasites, and characterized by invasions into the tendons and, clinically, by gastrointestinal symptoms, fever, and eruptions on the head. Contracted by the ingestion of undercooked pork.

How I Transcended Trichinosis

The name of the beauty shop was Janja, which means "little lamb."
Though the name doesn't exactly inspire confidence, it's easy
to remember and pronounce: Jan-ja. It's just a hole in the wall,
originally built as a foyer where the tenants could chat. An agreement
was made with the tenants, a few renovations took place, and,
voilà—a beauty salon! Janja. Two hair dryers, two shifts, no breaks.

The hairdresser, also named Janja, had small children at home.
Her thoughts were always elsewhere—on dinner or clean clothes
for the day. She was dead on her feet. Sometimes, for relaxation, she
would visit with her customers: Who was ill? Who was soon to kick
the bucket? Whose children were ungrateful brats?

"Tragedy, tragedy. And it's getting worse," Janja would say as
you leafed through an old magazine. "More and more customers
are suffering from eruptions on the head, which is one of the sure
symptoms. They pop up everywhere, at any time, and that's what is
so terrifying. Sometimes they spread over the entire eye."

Janja had firsthand information. All the women sitting under the
adjustable hair dryers would agree with Janja that *it* had arrived on
my head.

I was taken to the head of the line for my haircut. Janja isn't one
of those hairdressers who has the habit of saying out loud, "Oh,
your head has such a strange shape," or "Have you gone and cut
your own hair since I saw you last?" or "After I do you, I'll have to
go find some gypsy to sharpen up my scissors." No, not at all. Janja
takes care of every head, whether it's a big potato-head or a tiny
bird-sized noggin, whether perfectly round or oblong, inflated like

a balloon or pinched in places even the Almighty could not have anticipated. *The shape of your head is your business and nobody else's!* That's Janja's motto. But if it is a man's head, then only a pompadour would do.

"A pompadour," Janja would say, "is never out of fashion." Even in these diseased times, when heads assume the most unusual shapes, Janja always recommends a pompadour. Combine this with a pompadour Christmas special—how could I refuse?

The problem is that after a few scissor snips, layer by layer, my face feels oddly exposed. This happens every time. I rarely look up while my hair is being cut. It's not a matter of principle, but the suspense about what I will see when I look in the mirror. I watch as the hair piles up on the floor. I listen to the scissors—*click, click, click.* Then the trimmers and the bent scissors for the bangs. The end is near. I usually reject the gel. All in all, chances are that at Janja's nobody will pay you the slightest attention. Like I said—small children, dinner, a big hairdresser's heart.

But this wasn't my day.

"Oh, your hairline has receded again!"

This time she couldn't help herself. I was laid bare. Janja's voice quivered. I had the feeling she was trying to remain calm and collected, and I was grateful for that.

"And on your forehead area, in case you haven't noticed," she added politely, soulfully. She would have shown the same delicacy toward a husband who had slapped her in a fit of anger. She was accustomed to suffering while she slaved over a hot stove.

Pay attention now: at that precise moment someone behind me slung a *Cosmo* to the floor. But Janja didn't want to cause a panic: "This ridge here—," she said as calmly as possible as she touched my upper forehead with her index finger. "This wasn't here the last time you came." Scuffling and shuffling ensued; it was the feet of the women under the hairdryers.

I wanted to tell her, "Well, that's obvious." But I kept quiet. My eyes were fixed on the hair.

"The left cheek," Janja continued. "Please look toward the mirror!"

There was an obvious bulge. It could be seen by the naked eye.

Some people are narcissistic and love to stare at themselves in the mirror, devouring everything they think is special about their face in one greedy look. Clients like this have a closer relationship with their hairdressers, who, in return, turn a blind eye to new developments on their heads. As a matter of fact, studies show that the face changes its appearance several times every day. So big deal. All I wanted was to reap the benefits of the pompadour Christmas special. I wished she'd make it snappy.

"You think I'm imagining things." Janja tried to force my cooperation, holding the open scissors in one hand and the tweezers in the other. "It looks like something's popped out at your temples, young man!"

"This ridge here—," Janja rotates me around in the chair until I am facing the women, then she runs her finger over my cheekbones. "This ridge wasn't here the last time I cut his hair." She was addressing a certain woman under the hairdryer.

"Hmmmm."

"Do you see what I see? I mean the swelling on the cheek."

"Look, Janja, he's completely asymmetrical," the woman maliciously affirmed, her head covered with huge rollers. "He must have picked up some disease."

I knew they were exchanging looks above my head. The hairdryers were running on empty, because the other customers were already on their feet, heading toward the door, towels still wrapped around their heads.

"How long's the incubation period?" asked a voice accustomed to quick and precise answers. "Can it be passed on through the air? By touch? Get him out! I don't want to celebrate New Year's Eve with a caved-in head."

The woman who spoke was losing control, yet it was clear she didn't intend to leave with a wet head. Janja wanted to maintain the dignity of her profession—epidemics of trichinosis came and went, but customers remained, or survived, if you will. Janja lowered her voice to a whisper.

"Have you eaten any raw meat?" she whispered in my ear. I knew she was trying to protect me.

"I mean, any innards? You know as well as I do that they always throw in some raw meat from the draining sink when they slaughter the pigs. Am I right? You can tell me." She spoke in a confidential tone.

"Maybe some sausage? Right? You were eating some sausage?" interjected a woman with a perm in progress, watching for a sign of confirmation. "Look at him smirk, as though he doesn't give a damn about all the other heads."

Then things took a different turn. Janja picked up a strand of my hair with two fingers, ready to snip off half of it, her eyes darting mournfully along the wall, quick as a spider. She briefly rested her gaze on the crucifix hanging on the wall and the message affixed below it: *Peace be to this house.* Then, summoning her courage, she sentenced my cowlick to death. At the same time, in her characteristically slow voice, she sighed, "God help us."

The situation seemed to have calmed down. Two matrons sat back down under the hairdryers, legs crossed. The sound of pages being turned recommenced.

Janja got right to the point.

"Everyone asks why God would prohibit us from eating pork, especially since it's so tasty. But nobody asks whether He might just want to subject us to a new temptation, to see how great our love is, whether it has a price. If it does, I think giving up pork, because of a little bug in it, means we don't deserve to ever eat our fill again."

Meanwhile, she clipped off another tuft of hair.

She stepped back to view the cut in its entirety, but something was flaming, blazing, in her eyes.

"Just tell me this. Does anyone want to give up his traditions? The French eat moldy cheese. Every holiday appetizer plate has moldy cheese on it. You think those fat oil men from Texas would give up their bloody steaks because of some mad cow disease? Never!"

She picked up a hairdryer, holding it like a Colt 45.

"That's the way our people are; they're always looking for a reason to reject their heritage," Janja warned before the hairdryer drowned her out. The poor thing. She was filled with what, under different conditions, would be characterized as pride.

And then, between the blasts of the hairdryer, I heard her words rotating around my head, as though they were being delivered by a doomed soul from the highest peak of some holy mount.

"Don't stop. Don't give up eating pork. You'll always get a discount here, and I'll always take you ahead of the line. Just let me know if you don't want a pompadour, it's OK. Someday we'll find a haircut that does justice to your head. You'll never go bald, I guarantee you. But don't give it up. Keep on eating just like before. God sees everything—suffering is what makes men heroes." And so she continued, until the very last swipe of the comb.

I have to admit that the pompadour was first-class. Janja refused to charge me. She lacked the words to express what I had, at that moment, represented to her. Agitated, she moved to the corner and wiped her hands with a towel. She was having a tough time. As I left the salon, two women were standing quietly, and Janja's scissors were clicking behind me, in perfect rhythm with my steps.

I realized that some kinds of love never die.

Generation of Talented Experts

The year 1990 was full of portents of the imminent catastrophes of war. A quiet summer night would suddenly be cut through by a loud volley of gunshots. Tanks could be seen creeping through the forest, silent as vampires. Women became hysterical and fell into fits of jealous delirium at parties and gatherings, turning on their husbands, and often with a cake knife. Men talked politics, drowned themselves in alcohol by night, and by day invested feverishly in Lotto tickets. The infrastructure collapsed quickly. An epoch was coming to a permanent end; this was obvious to everyone. These years were characterized by a high rate of divorce in marriages that had previously appeared stable. In this story I wanted to illustrate a moment when a man leaves his secure home, together with the state in which he lives, and enters a new time-space vacuum.

G.N. ✚

Generation of Talented Experts

The old Tree Trunk motels were, as a rule, built near larger cities throughout the former state, yet far enough away to maintain the illusion of having left home. There was usually some kind of memorial forest—a wooded preserve named in honor of a Communist functionary or some other historical figure—with a gas pump out front and a side street that led to the motel parking lot. The front part of the motel was constructed with a huge glass surface, but the one-way glass from the outside looking in guaranteed the privacy of those inside, as did the inside "intimate bar," whose aquarium with its silent fish contributed to the overall atmosphere. The lights in the bar were orange, and they played those interminable Muzak songs. The tactful waiters rarely emptied the ashtrays. Here a man could rehash the past, contemplate its significance, and think long and hard about his next steps. In the jargon of the time that had just run its course, these were people at a turning point in their lives.

Guests on their own were betrayed by small details such as haphazardly tied neckties or mud spatters on their pantcuffs; unshaved cheeks dotted with purple cloudlets of broken capillaries. Various middle-aged people came in and out continuously. Judging by the tips they left, it was clear that money was no problem.

Sometimes they would jerk all of a sudden, turn right and left, take a deep drag on their cigarettes, drink their coffee down to the dregs, then assume their previous pose. It seemed they were waiting for something, some resolution.

Geli spent his first day away from home in a corner of this "intimate bar" trying to recover from a heavy lunch. He was overwhelmed by feelings of apathy, yet he tried to resist them in light of the stultifyingly slow pace at which the afternoon was passing.

And then, shortly before dusk, a white limousine appeared behind the gas station. Through the window, Geli watched it slowly circle the parking lot. Only when he recognized the license plate did he react. Geli gave a sign to the head bartender. He was one of the good old boys, trustworthy and impeccably well groomed. Geli turned from him to observe the car in which three hefty individuals were apparently conducting last-minute consultations before getting out. One of them was Geli's wife. The bartender discarded his dishtowel, untied his apron, and adjusted his work blazer. Geli passed quickly by him as he headed toward the back exit.

The walk through the woods to the bungalow did him good. Judging by the cool current of air, he guessed the river to be very close, maybe just beyond the hedge. He passed most of the ticky-tacky cottages. His was in the last row. He knocked and entered a bare-walled space. He removed his shoes, got comfortable, opened the water spigots to let them run a little, then barked out a manly gob of spit. His face moist, he threw off his coat. Already he regretted not having brought along a sweatsuit, as the sheets were cold and the blankets itchy. He stretched out in his suit pants and turned on the portable TV. He gulped down two sleeping tablets and, before falling asleep, succeeded in watching part of the European baton-twirling championships.

Geli was awakened by a scream and breaking glass. Someone was crashing through the bushes around the cottage. All at once he heard quickened breathing under the window, then the sound of running feet. He lay motionless. His eyes slowly adjusted to the dark, while in his mind he reviewed all the dangers that the forest, the night, and the unstable political situation might present. He had taken none of this into consideration when he rented the bungalow.

He crept to the door in his stocking feet and, holding his breath, listened long and hard before slowly opening it. The forest shimmered in the full moonlight.

"Hey!" someone called out to him in a muffled voice. A man with a protruding forehead peered out from the decorative hedge.

"Did you see them?" he whispered.

"What am I supposed to have seen?" Geli answered mistrustfully. The guy was taken aback. "Well—aren't we on the same side?"

"Good night," Geli said, abruptly ending the conversation and crawling back into bed. He tried in vain to get back to sleep, but it seemed as though the hands of the clock were stuck on four. He could hardly wait to hear the sound of birds chirping and the distant roar of trucks on the main highway.

Dawn finally broke. He began thinking about water for coffee, which, if he were home, he would already have put on to boil. He missed his half hour by the radio, leafing through yesterday's newspapers, then going to the bathroom to shave while everyone else was still asleep. He was overcome again with listlessness, the strongest since he had left. But a frightful banging at the door suddenly demanded his attention.

"Who is it?" he yelled out from his bed.

"Neighbor." The frail voice reminded him of the little man in the early morning hours. He was not mistaken. At his door stood the little man, wearing only his pants with a jacket pulled over his bare chest, shaking imperceptibly after an apparently sleepless night. His index finger was pointed in an indeterminate direction.

"Would you be so kind as to squeeze me out a little toothpaste?"

Geli nodded benevolently, perhaps because the night before he had been so abrupt with the man.

"Toothpaste, toothpaste," he hummed as he rifled through his Adidas bag. He was sure he had bought some yesterday at the gas station.

"Aha, here it is, son of a bitch."

Geli gallantly squeezed a thick line onto his neighbor's index finger. The man thanked him and went back to his bungalow across the way.

The rear window of the man's bungalow was broken. As Geli watched him depart, he thought how sad it was when people of that age were forced to sponge toothpaste. At the entrance, the man turned around, and Geli, confused by his look, retreated into the house. *To fix a window like this one won't be cheap!* he thought.

His biggest task today would be to call the personnel office and report his absence at work. At first he was going to claim emergency family matters, which was not far from the truth. He was planning to take three days off, maybe five to make it a whole week, so he could prepare for the first court appearance.

But it was still early morning, and he couldn't really pull himself together yet.

He took an inventory of the clothes he had in his bag. Under these circumstances, every object seemed particularly precious. He smoothed out an extra shirt and hung it up to keep it clean and orderly for the court proceeding. His pants were wrinkled from having slept in them. Geli began thinking seriously about an iron. This time the knocks on his door were deafening.

"Geli, open up. It's me, Srnec!"

Srnec, Srnec—he racked his brain but found it completely blocked. The fact that someone was calling out his name concerned him, since he wished to be incognito here at the motel. But what else could he do?

He opened up and saw Renato Srnec standing on the porch.

"Oh, it's you!" Almost before he had finished speaking, Srnec shoved him inside.

"Lock the door," Srnec said, ignoring Geli's outstretched hand. Srnec didn't relax until Geli locked the door.

"What are you doing here?" Geli was genuinely surprised. "Haven't you and Goca already—"

Srnec grimaced. "We had a successful court-facilitated reconciliation after—"

"Oh, I see." It all seemed clearer to Geli now.

"It came and went," Srnec jested. "Nobody will ever talk me into doing that again," he hastened to tell Geli. "After the reconciliation, all hell broke loose."

Geli went over to the chair and started going through his things.

"And what's happening with you?" Srnec's mood had suddenly improved. "I thought at least you and Josipa had a solid marriage," he said ironically.

But already, in the next moment, his attention was directed elsewhere. He walked over to the window and pulled back the curtains.

"What's going on?" Geli asked.

Srnec was concentrating on something outside the window.

"You just got here yesterday, right?" Srnec asked him sternly. Geli looked away.

"Pull yourself together, man," Srnec warned, moving away from the window. "I watched you strutting around on the porch last night with that nitwit across the way."

"Geli," he said, raising his voice and looking him in the eye, "forget that you're out here in the country! Your wife, her relatives, who knows who else, they're disturbing the guests here! Things are still hot, still in limbo, you know?" Geli realized that Srnec still held a grudge against him for his impulsive remarks on the porch.

"So, what did this guy across the way want?" asked Srnec.

"Toothpaste."

Srnec twitched. His thoughts seemed to be racing. Then he smiled.

"Toothpaste, haha. That's really unbelievable."

"What's so funny?" Geli was getting irritated.

"They jumped him while he was sleeping," Srnec spat out, rotating his head as though to relieve tension. "He got away from them through the window in the nick of time, haha!" Srnec moved to the window again and checked out the terrain.

"Don't forget!" he said, measuring Geli from head to toe. "Don't forget that everyone's armed these days!"

Geli agreed, and Srnec gave him a benevolent look.

"The motel has a registration book," Geli remarked lackadaisically. Everyone's registered in it, right?"

"My dear friend, people working in this motel know what they're doing. Everything has its price." Srnec reached over and took an apple he spotted lying on top of Geli's bag.

They decided to go to lunch together.

Srnec made his escape through the door first, then as agreed, he cleared his throat three times from underneath the porch. Geli rushed out and quickly locked the door behind him. Partly hunkered down as they ran, they crossed the open field and moved deeper into the forest. Neither one of them spoke.

Judging from the condition of Srnec's clothing, Geli concluded he had been away from home for quite a while.

They entered the motel through the boiler room. Geli tried to be as tactful as possible. "You know, your suit is in pretty bad shape."

Srnec straightened out his jacket and brushed hair from his shoulders. "That's probably true," he said. "I didn't have time to take anything else out of the apartment."

"Was there a huge commotion when you left?" Geli asked this innocently, but Srnec got right into his face. The boiler was steaming. Geli could feel Srnec's shallow breathing.

"She shot at me," he said dryly. "With a Beretta. I could file charges, but fuck it. There aren't any witnesses."

Geli trembled. He had a different recollection of Srnec's wife, Goca, who worked at the school, if his memory served him correctly. Back then, they went out on double dates. He recalled Goca as a simple little woman who preferred to sit quietly in a crowd.

"I told you everything went to hell after the court-ordered reconciliation attempt," Srnec said.

"Jaysus." Geli sounded shaken. "What the hell is happening to us?"

"There's going to be war," Srnec spat out, shoving open the iron door in front of him.

The boiler control room had three small tables pushed together. The air was heavy, and pipes of different sizes pressed upon them from all directions.

Srnec yawned. "Lately I've been feeling most comfortable right here in the boiler room," he remarked. He pushed a chair over to Geli. "I hardly ever go up to the 'intimate bar.' I just don't want to take the risk." After saying this he rapped three times on one of the pipes hanging down from the ceiling.

"So what do you want to eat?" he asked Geli, who was still feeling unsettled.

"You want eggs? Soft or hardboiled?"

"Soft," Geli answered absently.

Srnec rapped on another pipe five times. At least that's how many times Geli counted.

"A little ham on the side, huh?"

Geli shrugged. He heard several hollow thumps.

"Coffee or tea?"

"Coffee," Geli answered, straining.

Srnec knocked once more, this time on the widest pipe. The waiter from the previous day's shift came quickly down the steep stairs with their breakfast. He gave them a hearty greeting, smiling warmly at Geli, the newcomer.

He made a quick comment about the events of the night before: "Unfortunately, these things happen," he said, brushing the table off with his hand. Then he turned to Geli and said in a more official tone, "This concerns you!"

He poured coffee into a glass and spoke. "Last night I had a short conversation with your wife. Allow me to remark that she was in a very poor state and asked me to provide her with the number of your bungalow." He offered Geli a cup. Geli turned pale.

"Of course," continued the waiter, "I told her you were not here unless you had registered under a phony name. You know," he said, clearing his throat, "sometimes even we can't afford to get involved. We still have hotel regulations to observe. You understand?"

"Of course, thank you," Geli said. Srnec had already made an attack on the food.

"No problem, discretion and trust are the trademarks of this motel. But," Srnec said haltingly, "as far as her parents, your father-in-law and mother-in-law are concerned—"

Geli looked as though he'd been overcooked.

"They don't seem like the type of people who'd make problems. You know, I have a nose for this," he said.

"Oho, you lucky guy, you," Srnec said, his mouth stuffed with food, and he gave Geli a kick under the table. Geli quickly took out his wallet and handed the waiter several bills.

They returned to the bungalow through the forest, the same way they'd come.

Srnec pulled a flask out from somewhere. A foul odor emanated from it.

"It's too early for schnapps!" Geli said glumly, as he picked burrs off his socks.

Srnec took a big swallow and wiped his mouth with his glove. "I can tell you haven't been away from home long!"

Srnec paced the room silently. It seemed that Geli's attitude made him anxious. Then he took off his jacket and swayed back and forth with his hands in his pockets.

"You know what the trouble is with our generation?" he asked.

Geli just shrugged his shoulders.

"The problem is," he said, "that we're resistant to change. We've failed as a generation on this issue."

Srnec gave him a little punch on the shoulder afterward, man to man, trying to lift his spirits.

"And you know," Geli continued, "young girls would kill for men of our caliber." He let out a long sigh and retreated to the corner of the room.

"I'm talking about real women who value what we have to offer: maturity, charm, a college diploma, and a good salary," he said. "Those are some of our strongest weapons. We need to activate the damn potential of our generation!"

Srnec again pulled the flask out of his coat pocket and waved it in Geli's direction.

"And such girls do exist," he said meaningfully. "But it's not so easy to make contact with them," he concluded mysteriously.

"Ah, what the hell!" Srnec raised the flask. "To your health!"

Geli finally began to show a little life. He raised his head.

"Are you trying to tell me something?" he asked.

Then Srnec became nervous all of a sudden.

He scraped his muddy shoe along the floor. His eyes skittered around the room. It seemed that something had shattered inside him.

"Okay, okay, all right," he said, as though he were falling apart at the seams. "Whatever!"

"Whatever, Geli, whatever you want!" he repeated, giving him a veiled look. "Just be ready at five!" he warned. "I'm taking you with me!"

Moving toward the door, Srnec appeared to be carried away by some invisible force.

"Then see you at five," he said, closing the door behind him.

Geli immediately rushed to the window. He watched Srnec as he walked quickly over the cleared field then spun around before he reached the next row of cottages. He gave Geli a poisonous smile.

"Moron!" said Geli, throwing himself down on the bed.

At exactly five o'clock, Srnec was waiting for him in front of the porch.

A few minutes later, they were making tracks through the woods. Srnec kept rushing him along.

"Step it up! People value punctuality!"

Geli was becoming more and more nervous, which he attributed to the bad schnapps, the sleazy motel room, and being away from home for so long.

Srnec had brought his greasy hair under some sort of control. It also seemed to Geli that he had changed his shirt and scraped the mud off his shoes and socks.

"Hey, now you look a lot better," Geli offered as a compliment. Srnec was gasping from lack of breath.

A car had been hidden in the bushes, near the grassy riverbank. Judging by the tire indentations, Geli had concluded that Srnec left the car there on a regular basis.

Together they brushed the leaves off the hood. "The car's absolutely safe here," said Srnec, as an afterthought.

"Would Goca really do something to it?" Geli asked in feigned astonishment.

Srnec did not respond.

It was very difficult to extricate the car from the mud. They drove up onto the road and headed toward town. Srnec drove in spurts or jerks, letting the motor grind along in low gear. He stopped at a flower stand and quickly returned with a bouquet, which he put on Geli's lap.

"It's worth the money," he said, driving off.

As they rumbled through the center of town, Srnec's mood suddenly turned dark.

He began to mutter out loud, "You pitiful idiots, slime, losers!" He gaped around him with an expression of deep disgust.

"I recognize them by the way they walk! Man, the town is full of them!" he sputtered.

"Look, over there, another trained monkey!" He thrust his chin toward a man crossing the street. "Look at him, he's probably hurrying home to the little woman so she can slap him around. You wanna bet?"

Srnec slammed on the brakes, as though stopping to let the man cross the street. He rolled down the window and shamelessly stuck his head halfway out.

"Hey, there, Mr. Pussywhipped!" he yelled out. Geli covered his face with the flowers.

"Admit that you're going home to keep the little woman company while she cooks her pot of soup. Go on!" he called out. "Hurry home so you can help her chop the carrots, make yourself useful!"

Srnec's hoarse laugh was drowned out by the motor. He stepped on the gas. As they were leaving town he held forth about vampirous women who had taken over the entire generation, the men who had surrendered to them, and the terror they voluntarily endured. He was absolutely in his element.

"You know," he said at one point, "I can't wait for the war to start." He allowed the sentence to reverberate throughout the car, a smug look on his face. Then he turned to Geli.

"Just to break the monotony," he explained. But Geli was ignoring him, suddenly massaging his own temples. Srnec retreated into silence.

They turned off onto a narrow road and drove for a while over the thickets. They snorted in disgust when they entered a town so small that it didn't even have a signpost. Srnec slowed down and looked into the houses on the right side of the road. Suddenly he slammed on the brakes and backed up to a bridge.

They got out. At the gate, Srnec wiped his shoes on his pantleg. He regarded Geli.

He called out a name, then he said, "You could at least have fixed yourself up a bit."

They heard quick steps. A plump woman of advanced years cried out softly and embraced Srnec below the waist. He held out the bouquet.

"You shouldn't have wasted your money!" she told him mournfully.

Srnec signaled to Geli over the woman's tidy bun.

They went into the dining room. The table was set with double plates and beautiful silverware. It smelled like a roast was in the oven. Srnec introduced Geli as a colleague from work.

"He's an expert on electronic databases," he offered. The woman silently considered Geli then excused herself for a moment.

Embroidered towels hung from the walls, and every shelf was covered with snow-white cloths. Srnec stretched out on the sofa in the corner of the room and lit a cigarette.

"Ugh!" he exhaled, unbuttoning his top shirt button. Geli

pretended a keen interest in the rustic objects displayed around the room. He touched the steam iron and the ancient weaving mill with its sharp awl. He let his eyes roam over all the handmade items. By then the hostess had returned with schnapps and a light snack. She served part of it onto the plates then sat down on the couch next to Srnec. She spiked an hors-d'oeuvre with a toothpick and put it into his mouth. Srnec's hands hung over both sides of the sofa. He regarded Geli with a kingly air as he chewed vigorously.

Then he pointed to the schnapps. The woman put down the snack plate and reached to the edge of the table for a glass, then put it to his lips. Srnec patted her on the back as she poured schnapps down his throat.

Srnec wailed: "It's so strooooonnnnng! Aaaargh!!"

And then a girl came into the room.

Srnec momentarily rid himself of the plate; the toothpick hung suspended in the air. Srnec approached the girl, his shoulders swinging. She cast her eyes downward in confusion. Srnec smiled and brushed back a strand of hair from her face. The hostess quickly disappeared into the kitchen, her hands clasped around her apron.

They could hear her saying something from the kitchen.

"A little louder!" Srnec called to her as he pulled out a chair for the girl.

As she came out with a roast, the hostess looked over at the girl.

"You need to eat now," she told her. The girl covered the empty plate with both her hands.

"I don't know what to do with her," the hostess complained to Srnec. "All day long she picks at her food. Just covers her plate and feels sorry for herself," she said in desperation. Then she sat down between Srnec and her daughter. "But you've got to admit—those eyes, hah?"

Srnec moved back a bit in order to better observe the girl's eyes.

"And those voluptuous lips, hah?" said the mother, as she wiped her glistening forehead with the dishcloth.

"I don't hear you, Srnec. You're not sufficiently taken by her charms."

Srnec took a huge bite.

"Right now I'm admiring the mother who has produced such a daughter," he said. Geli was thinking to himself that Srnec sounded like someone who had flunked out of a defunct school of etiquette. Besides that, he came across as a toastmaster or something. The way he extricated a bone from his mouth, the way he raised his glass. This was after they'd moved on to wine and mineral water.

"Child, at least take a little wine," her mother urged. The girl made an ill-tempered grimace, after which her mother extended her arms in a gesture of helplessness.

"She acts like she's got a hair up her behind," the mother said angrily. "She takes after her late father. He was always grumbling, and you never knew what was on his mind."

She pulled the girl up by the hands. "Come on, cheer up a little!"

The girl recovered her hands and cupped her chin in them.

The meal slowly came to an end. At first the wine had arrived in big plastic bottles; when that was gone, the glass bottles began lining up, one, two, three. When the clock struck ten, the girl excused herself and retreated to her room.

Srnec turned to Geli: "That's what you call a good upbringing," he slurred. He drank a bit more, then his chest heaved and he returned the last gulp back into the glass, spitting out a little along the way. He lay down on the sofa, mumbling something about life in the village, a ranch, animals, and living off the land. It didn't sound very persuasive.

The hostess returned with a watermelon cut into slices.

She sat down on the edge of the sofa and began removing seeds with a knife. She placed the finished slices into his mouth. Srnec squinted and ate until the juice began to run down his chin. On several occasions he attempted to sing a song, but the melody soon petered out. It was late and Geli insisted that they be on their way. Srnec reached his arms out to the woman, who pulled him up with surprising strength and set him firmly on his feet.

He burped at an inopportune moment, directly in the woman's face. One eyelid steadfastly refused to open.

Geli grabbed him by the elbow and pointed him toward the door.

On the porch, Srnec sought in vain for words of gratitude. The moon was so full that it seemed unlikely to survive the dawn. Geli hoped Srnec would not notice the moon. He felt somehow that if he did, the problems would proliferate.

But Srnec looked straight ahead as they approached the car.

He felt both the car and the lock. The woman stood next to him, lighting matches one after the other so that he could find the keys more easily.

"Ma'am," he simpered, "please give my greetings—ah forget the greetings, kiss her for me."

Geli elbowed him in the ribs to focus his attention.

"Let me finish!" Srnec growled. "Kiss her—" he attempted to finish the sentence but suddenly gave up, turned on the motor, and gave a quick goodbye honk of the horn.

He drove slowly, his nose almost pressed against the windshield.

"Fuck it," Srnec muttered. "I couldn't remember the girl's name. What an idiot I am. I forgot her name."

"Everything will be all right. Just keep your eyes on the road," Geli said, attempting to calm him.

"Bullshit, it'll be all right! This is a big minus for me!"

Then he turned to Geli. "Do you think the woman realized I didn't know the girl's name?"

"Well, who are you trying to seduce?" Geli asked him. "The mother or the daughter?"

Geli felt Srnec's impatience toward him growing. Srnec shot him a dark look that Geli was unable to decipher. But in spite of the fog and the state he was in, Srnec deftly avoided the potholes in the road.

"Sorry," said Geli.

Srnec looked stiffly ahead.

The memorial forest appeared as an imperceptibly darker spot on the black horizon. The bushes were scraping against the back bumper. Geli made comments now and then to Srnec, but he, still insulted, remained silent. Visibility decreased as they penetrated deeper into the forest. The surface of fog transformed the headlights into whorls of steam. Suddenly a hand appeared on the windshield. There was a dull thud. Srnec braked amateurishly and the car swerved. They slid into something soft, and the motor died.

Geli immediately said that it made no sense to flee, but Srnec remembered a hammer that should have been under the car seat. He bent over.

"There are two of us," he said with bravado. They heard deep voices around them. A military flashlight from outside hit them in the eyes.

Srnec dug his feet into the floor. He didn't want to get out of the car. Geli watched him with pity as he resisted the strong arms that were pulling him out.

As far as Geli was concerned, they didn't need to yank him out. He got out by himself. He was shoved against the car then roughly searched. At first he couldn't see anyone's face, but he felt a metal barrel being pressed into his flesh. All he could hear was Srnec insisting that they had made a mistake. Both their faces were silently checked with a flashlight. Meanwhile, a tractor with an open cabin approached.

The driver stayed seated. He turned off the motor.

The moon appeared above the forest, a bit more deformed than before. Both Geli and Srnec were shoved toward the tractor operator, who had just emerged from the bushes.

"It's not either of them, Daddy," said a voice.

"I told you you were making a mistake," Srnec whined.

The tractor operator was not to be moved. The moonlight made him look dashing. He rested his elbows on the steering wheel and lit a cigarette. The others stood and patiently waited.

He exhaled voluminously. "All my life I worked hard to feed my children," he said contemplatively. He spit on the wet, dark ground, then he went on in an even more cantankerous tone.

"I raised them with my own two hands, as respectable people. I took care of them, made sure they had a good life—I even came up with a respectable dowry for my only daughter. Not even a big city girl would have been ashamed of the dowry my daughter took that Mr. Fancypants."

He shook the ash from his cigarette. "Come on, Jule, tell these city gentlemen what Dolores brought with her."

"Household appliances and money," said a voice from the dark.

"How much was it all worth?"

"At least 20,000, Dad."

The man laughed heartily. "You said it, Jule, at least that much!"

"And what did Mr. Hotshot do in return?"

His voice thundered through the forest, frightening a deer in the nearby bushes. One of the boys shot off a gun. In the silence that followed, Geli observed Srnec, sniveling quietly.

The tractor operator suddenly concluded he had wasted too much precious time. He turned on the motor. Looking over his shoulder, he addressed them one more time:

"Nobody escapes from the mountain warriors!" he called out as he cranked the steering wheel powerfully and disappeared into the brush.

Two men jumped onto the tractor, one on each side. A third sat on the trailer. The tractor crossed the canal, crushing the foliage as it penetrated into the forest.

Srnec rushed to the car.

"It got stuck in the last rut after all," he said, as he kicked the wheel furiously. He undid his tie and crammed it into his pocket. Fog from the river had turned the night icy.

Geli flipped up the collar of his jacket. The cold had somehow penetrated up from below, through his legs. He wrapped himself in his arms. His legs began to twitch uncontrollably. He felt close to a nervous breakdown.

They set out on foot. Amid deafening silence they came upon the first bungalows. All the windows were dark.

"Here we'll part ways," Srnec announced. Geli was enraged.

"Just like that? After all we've been through?"

Srnec didn't turn back, just kept going straight ahead. In fact, he began to run and disappeared into the darkness.

"Dickhead!" Geli spat out.

He found it incredibly difficult to move from his spot.

He had seen scenes like this in movies, where the guy is alone at the end, usually underneath some bridge or on a wide, dark avenue. The problem was that it was the end of the movie, and you never found out what happened to the hero. There was only some vague supposition that he had managed to preserve his dignity. *So what happens after the last credits run out?* Geli asked himself. *Maybe the guy did go to some river and wait for the sun to come up.* Sleepless nights could sometimes clarify the situation. This thought resurrected some long-forgotten traditional pearl of wisdom. Many had probably tried this before, but without results. Besides, in his generation, sleepless nights meant a loss, something that had to be recovered later.

But now that he thought about it, Geli realized he had nothing to recover. He dragged himself toward the bungalow.

All his days from now on were going to be like this, he thought. He would probably need less sleep than before. He would feed himself irregularly, only when he managed to rustle up something. First he would lose his gut, and then the fat on his buttocks. He would finally have a flat ass, he thought—he knew some women liked men with small asses—and then he could discard all his suits and go back to wearing jeans. This line of thought pleased him considerably.

He climbed up to the porch. At one point he had added to his wardrobe a hip-length jacket that was supposedly more flattering to one's overall figure. He reflected that no one would be around any longer to lecture him about his appearance.

And finally, he needed to sharpen his facial structure, so he would, at an opportune moment, start wearing sideburns. In time, he would more and more resemble Joe Strummer. The mature Joe Strummer, of course, with sideburns halfway down his face.

He unlocked the door to the bungalow.

Geli burned with the desire to see himself in five, ten years. Then, he thought, he would probably recall with a superior air everything that had happened tonight—his struggle for privacy, sleeping in a strange bed in wrinkled pants, the mud seeping into his shoes and squishing between his frozen toes.

In five, ten years…

He crept into bed, quiet as a mouse, and positioned his head on his clasped palms.

He decided that at all costs he must remain on good terms with his wife. That was after all the trend. Post-nuptial friendship—that's what the developed world called having a friendly, stress-free cup of coffee with your ex. Lately, he had begun asking himself what the secret was of the good, well-maintained skin you saw on people in the West. Now, here in the bungalow, the explanation suddenly dawned on him: an "understanding" between partners removes stress.

Oh, how Geli had been longing for civilization, for Europe to finally arrive!

And the nation has made its decision, he mused. More and more often he noticed license plates carrying the blue stickers of the European Union. He didn't know why, but he had the idea those stickers were being distributed free of charge somewhere. Maybe at gas stations? He intended to ask about this—he would ask tomorrow when he went to buy razor blades.

Then he heard a gunshot, and immediately afterward, an echo resounding through the trees. When he perched up on one elbow, he heard a scratching sound against the door. His hearing was suddenly attuned to outside sounds. He got up carefully. Someone was at the doorstep.

So it had come to this: either open the door or go back to bed. He knew he could no longer ignore what was happening around him. If that were the case, he would never have left home. It was as though Geli had experienced some kind of release. He opened the door.

The man from the bungalow across the way fell dead across his bare feet. Later he realized this had been a key event in his life.

Behind him, in the clearing, the tractor was making a full revolution. Dark figures, their faces in shadow, undulated along its powerful, exposed haunches. There was a smell of spent gunpowder.

Europe seemed easily within reach in those years. Everything was coming up roses. The morning breeze brought the scent of water. It was so hard to stop hoping.

Three Kings Day

I'd be lying if I said keeping one's gallstones in a dish above the television was a Croatian national custom, but I have been in a lot of houses and apartments where the inhabitants have patted themselves on the back over their gallstones. My grandfather, I recall, kept them in a porcelain dish; above the television, of course. They were sharp and irregularly shaped (like small corals), and as I held them in my hand, I would try to imagine the pain my grandfather had so stoically endured because of them. This story is an attempt to answer the question, "Why do these people take so much pride in their affliction?"

G.N. ✚

Three Kings Day

Bojko felt an indefinite tingling in his stomach area, like an itch, but he continued to watch the New Year's Eve program on television. At the stroke of midnight, he hauled himself out of bed, turned up the volume, and uncorked the champagne. He hadn't decorated the house in ages; since his sister had gotten married, he barely even remembered where the ornaments and angel hair were kept. He had always had trouble choosing a Christmas tree, anyway, so the spare atmosphere of the sitting room didn't really bother him. He had forced himself to buy champagne, though he realized as he poured it that he had purchased kiddie champagne—non-alcoholic.

Right after he took the first sip, a strong jolt of pain coursed through his body. He gripped the edge of the table with both hands. The television host was announcing a spot about the extravagant events of the evening when Bojko became seriously concerned about his condition. He tried to lean back against the couch, but the pain forced him into a squatting position. His left flank began to throb. He heard himself groan and suddenly felt the coolness of the floor tiles on the tip of his nose. He rolled over on his side, his vision fogged by stabs of pain. *Is this going to go on forever?* he thought. At one point, he succeeded in grabbing the telephone cord with his foot, after which the telephone tumbled to the floor, within his reach. He made a connection, waited for two further attacks to pass, then dialed 911.

He was operated on the next morning.

He came to in the recovery room on the first afternoon of the New Year. The room was quiet and dimly lit. A few hours later,

the on-duty nurse made her rounds. The following day, the same
nurse presented him with a plastic box inscribed with his name and
containing his six gallstones. This was the hospital's regular practice.

During visiting hours, his sister Kata showed up with her son
Dodo, Bojko's nephew. He mentioned the gallstones to them.

"Here they are," Bojko said, taking them out from under the
pillow. His sister smiled wanly while Dodo drank the juice that was
intended for Bojko. The kid managed to drink an entire liter and
eat at least a kilo of bananas without any reaction from Kata. Bojko
gloomily replaced the box under his pillow. During the night, he got
thirsty and became agitated, knowing the carton of juice was empty.

"Little bastard, piece of dog shit," Bojko complained, as though
Dodo could hear. He was horrified at the thought of drinking the
detestable hospital water until the day he was released.

No one was at home to take care of Bojko, who was a confirmed
bachelor. The first day, a house-call nurse came by to check on his
stitches. When he asked her to bring him a bottle of water, she was
surprised nobody was around to address his needs. Bojko didn't
know what to say.

Around two in the afternoon, he was shaken by a powerful thump
on the window that faced the street. Next, he heard the echo of
footsteps across the stone walkway, then another dull thud at his door.
His heart skipped a beat. Silence descended for several long moments.
Bojko stared, stunned, as the door opened. His nephew slipped
through the door. The boy's hair was freshly cut, down to the scalp, his
ears sprouting out on his square head. He settled his gaze on Bojko.

He pulled a stool over to his uncle's bed and roughly tore open a
plastic bag containing a pot. The smell of rice and milk wafted up,
and Bojko was suddenly famished.

"What about bread?" he asked the boy. "Did Mama send Uncle
some bread?"

Meanwhile, the boy had folded his hands on his groin and sat
motionlessly, contorting his face into hideous grimaces. A thread of
snot hung from one of his nostrils.

"Dodo, take some money from the drawer, and run down and get
some bread for Uncle, okay?"

Eyes narrowed, Dodo continued to stare at Bojko. He pulled his
head in toward his shoulders and twisted his mouth.

"Buy yourself some chocolate," Bojko cajoled. But his hunger had pushed him to start his meal without the bread.

The boy was obstinate and answered as though he were shooting the words from a big cannon: "Only if you give me the gallstones."

Bojko felt his wound gaping open fiendishly. At that moment he felt every stitch, ten in all—at least that's what they'd told him, though when his skin was stretched, he swore there were at least twelve to fifteen. *Doctors do make mistakes,* he thought as he watched his little nephew open drawers, one by one, insolently rooting through his uncle's things. Bojko pushed the pot of food away and replaced the lid. The sound of furniture being pushed around, the drawers thudding against the wood of the cabinet, made him want to curse, but instead, he let his head drop down on the pillow in despair.

A moment later, he looked around the room—the boy was nowhere to be seen. The door was closed, but a draft was coming from somewhere. He reached for the pot and finished off the cold rice. Only then did he remove the box of gallstones from under his pillow. First, he jiggled them against his ear—he wanted to hear them rattle; then he removed the pale blue lid.

He decided on the biggest gallstone, the size of a small fingernail, and rolled it between his fingers. He gauged its weight in the palm of his hand, smelled it, and finally, put it in his mouth and rolled it around gently, very gently. *This scoundrel,* he thought; *it must have been the chief culprit.* It had a sort of aerodynamic shape like a bullet. Bojko could imagine it rampaging like a vampire in his gall bladder on New Year's Eve, by its example encouraging the other stones to penetrate the thin membrane. He recalled the sharp stabs, resurrecting in his mind the intolerable pain even the old-timers avoided talking about after returning from the operating room.

His skin crawled.

As a boy, he had often peeked into the box containing his father's gallstones, which, according to his father's last wishes, had been buried with him. Now, three days after his own operation, Bojko remembered with nostalgia the round, smooth stones in the container, its lid decorated with shells.

His wound had almost stopped pinching. He felt satisfied that one more post-operative day was inching toward its end. He had to admit that he was plagued by hunger. This was the first time in his 36 years that he had had to be on a special diet. Until now, the word "diet" had been absent from his vocabulary. All his life, he had eaten in the only way appropriate for a real man—whenever he was hungry or whenever he smelled something tasty cooking in the oven and begging to be devoured. On such occasions, Bojko wouldn't hesitate to cut off a piece for himself, even though it wouldn't have hurt to go to bed on an empty stomach once in a while. His father—who ate a lot and often, even when it was better not to, and never went to bed hungry—served as his example in this regard.

He was just nodding off when he was struck by an epiphany: if he had gotten only six stones after an entire lifetime of heavy meals, then he could go ahead full throttle for the next 36 years and expect to get at least as many new ones. His body, he thought with satisfaction, was a highly efficient fat neutralizer. He replaced the lid on the container, put it back under his pillow, and turned on the television.

Early the next morning, his sister rushed in before work and brought him some Bambi Plasma protein cookies, the kind with extra nutrients. She informed him she had his lunch ready at home. "It's dietetic," she told him breathlessly.

"Don't send the boy over here anymore," he said in a weak voice. But apparently she didn't hear him, because Dodo showed up again around noon, with Bojko's lunch in a sack hanging from his wrist.

"Where are they?" he demanded as he entered, and he immediately started looking around the room.

"Come here, son—" Bojko tried to reason with him, but the boy, already practiced in this area, deftly yanked the blanket from his legs in one quick movement.

"Where'd you hide them?" he hissed.

Bojko wiggled his feet, rubbing his bare soles together in the unheated room. The boy kneeled down, took a flashlight out from somewhere, and lit up the space under the bed. Then he got up on his feet and slowly prowled around the room eyeing his uncle's furniture, as though deciding where to begin.

"Tell me where the gallstones are or you're not getting any lunch," the boy said, turning toward his uncle and pointing his index finger at him. For the first time since his attack, Bojko felt afraid of the little brat. He retreated to the upper half of the bed and closed his eyes, listening to the patter of little feet coming toward him.

The boy took the lunch sack and disappeared.

The winter sun attempted to penetrate the window. Dust motes quivering in the air charged insanely toward Bojko. His nephew quickly returned and without a word put the pot of soup down next to the bed. Bojko closed his eyes. He felt the boy's piercing gaze upon him, but couldn't figure out what he was up to. As soon as he heard the door hinge squeak closed, he breathed a sigh of relief and pulled the blanket up over his freezing feet.

He let a little time pass before he drew the edge of the curtain back as far as he could from his sitting position on the bed. He wanted to make sure Dodo was gone. Across the street, between the trees, he made out the hunched-over shape of his brother-in-law, a small, nervous, washed-out type with whom Bojko had never had anything in common. Dodo ran over to him and gesticulated for a few moments with his little hands. His father bent over, close to Dodo's square face. Dodo stepped back and pointed to the zipper of his pants, after which his father playfully boxed his ears. From a squatting position—above his son's shoulders—he contemplated Bojko's window then nodded. He got up and took his son's hand as they made their way down the brick walkway.

"Eh, so that's what's going on," Bojko said to himself. "My brother-in-law's in on it as well," he concluded, lowering himself carefully onto his pillow. "Why didn't I think of that right away?" he mumbled. His smile changed into a malicious grin.

He sipped the hearty soup right from the pot. It tasted a little sour for homemade soup. He stopped a few times and looked into the spoon, but continued eating until the last noodle was gone.

He rolled onto his back; his head was full of vague, swirling thoughts. He heard the kitchen pipes grumbling, announcing that the building's daily rhythms were coming to a close. Suddenly, he rolled over to the edge of the bed.

"Arrrgh, arrgh—" he groaned, burying his face in the feather pillow.

He tried not to think about it. Nonetheless, the taste of urine spread throughout his mouth. Just as he stuck his finger into his throat, the pain from his wound reminded him that he was not allowed to strain it. This was clearly written in the doctor's instructions: "Complete bed rest for the first week." Removal of the stitches, as Bojko figured it, would take place on Three Kings Day.

Later, while playing with his gallstones in an attempt to calm his nerves, he detected a barely perceptible growling in his intestines. Maybe Dodo hadn't pissed in the soup after all, he told himself, probing around in his mouth with the tip of his tongue in a search for traces of urine. All he managed to find were little bits of noodle between his teeth. By that evening, he almost didn't care whether or not Dodo had peed in the soup. He peeled two apples and ate them with the Bambi Plasma cookies, enjoying every bite, while somehow managing to suppress his longing for a slab of meat.

"If only I can hold out until Three Kings Day," he whispered to himself as he moved the stones around in his palm. Somehow, it excited him to think they had been in his gall bladder as recently as New Year's Eve.

Now they were here, in a container with his name written on it in black and white—concrete proof that they were his. Bojko pondered this long into the afternoon, then replaced the lid and gently shook the box again, just to hear the stones rattle one more time before he turned on the television. When the room grew dark, Bojko stuck the box under his pillow and said in a satisfied voice, "Ha, my brother-in-law! He can drop dead!"

Bojko expected further attacks, worse than the previous ones— maybe even during the night—but he vowed he'd much rather suffer than do without his gallstones.

A few days later, he thought he heard the horn of the Family Frost truck. The thought of fish, even frozen fish, made his mouth water. He put on his slippers as quickly as he could and, wallet in his pajama pocket, tottered on wobbly legs to the door. The moment he turned the key, the doorknob twisted in his hand, and Dodo barged into the room with a trumpet in his little fist. "Brrrrrumpapuuuuummmm!"

Bojko could barely keep his balance. The room began to spin. He took a deep breath and shook his head back and forth, barely managing to stay on his feet. The fresh air that burst in with Dodo had been too much for him.

Bojko realized he needed to react quickly, because the boy was already rooting through the bedclothes, the blanket, sheets, pillow— God almighty! When Dodo stuck his hand under the pillow, Bojko knew it was now or never and lunged toward the boy, who was already clutching the box of gallstones in one hand. He held the trumpet in the other as he stomped along the bed, tramping over the bedspread with his feet.

Bojko's sitting room was L-shaped, which at this moment was an advantage, because it made it harder for the boy to get around him. He spread his arms and slowly narrowed the space around his nephew. The mattress was squeaking excitedly. Bojko attributed this to the age of the bed. His elderly mother had died in this bed in her sleep. Shortly afterward, his father, on the same bed, had passed away after his second bout with gallstones.

But that was a long time ago, when he had been Dodo's age. Now, as he stalked the boy, it occurred to him that it was no wonder drugs abounded in the neighborhood, if small boys like Dodo were already jumping all over other people's beds, ready to steal their valuables or pee in their soup.

That's why our gallstones aren't round anymore, Bojko thought bitterly.

At all costs Bojko wanted to avoid raising his voice. He wanted to do this quietly. He was very close to his nephew; the boy's sweat made him smell like a small bird, a swallow perhaps. But the boy lurched to the side with all his strength, toward the cabinet, and Bojko was barely able to grab the back of his sweater. In retreat, Dodo turned to flee and deftly rolled on his hip over the armrest. Bojko cut him off, grabbed his ankle, and proceeded to liberate the box from his nephew's clenched fist.

There was no need to rush, so he opened Dodo's fingers slowly, one by one. Overcome by loathing yet trying to remain composed, he heard the joints crack. He trembled; his knees were weak, just as they had been on the day of the gall bladder attack. Dodo's moans took away Bojko's desire to cuff him at least once. He simply moved back, allowing Dodo to get back on his feet. The boy was limping but didn't complain. The copper trumpet was rolling across the floor. Bojko kicked it under the couch. BRRRrrrmm!

As soon as the sound of Dodo's footsteps in the yard died away, Bojko opened the transom window.

The winter sun reflected off the puddles in the street. He felt a breath of frosty air seep through his thin pajamas. He pulled back the curtains to better see outside. Dodo was moving along the house slowly, haltingly. A bit further, Bojko noticed the rear wheel of a Yugo 128. He couldn't make out the numbers on the license plate, but he knew it was his brother-in-law's by the bumper that was hanging off the car. Smoke billowed out of the muffler. The door was half-open, waiting for Dodo. A moment later, the car moved off without a sound.

It got dark early, so Bojko turned on the light. Indentations of small footprints were still on his bed sheets. He leaned against the cabinet, put his ear to the container, and shook it gently. One, two, three, four, five, six—he counted out all six gallstones.

That same night, he felt for a porcelain box deep in the cabinet. It was a long-forgotten souvenir with an idyllic scene painted on the lid. Inside were the remains of pieces of jewelry, a pearl or two, a broken brooch. He emptied it, brushed off the dust, and polished it with his sleeve. As he lay in bed, he realized how appropriate that box would be. He could display it anywhere, in any visible space— let's say, in the front of the cupboard or on the television. It looked like the kind of container a person would choose for valuables, and he wanted it to occupy a central spot. He carefully shook the stones out of the blue hospital container. They looked different in the porcelain box—prettier, fuller, livelier. His pulse slowed, and the dizziness he had felt from his previous efforts disappeared.

The next day, Dodo failed to appear. Bojko was careful not to let down his guard. All day long, he heard rustling sounds around the house. He checked the door and windows, set up a bar at the entrance from the attic stairs, and even inspected the chimney. He called his sister and reminded her that it was his Name Day.

"Oh!" Kata exclaimed. "Is today the feastday of Saint Gaspar, of the Three Kings?"*

"I'm completely flustered," she said. "Ever since this morning I've been so forgetful!" But Bojko was interested in only one thing: would she be coming tonight? "You're my brother. Of course we'll be coming—all three of us."

---

*   Gaspar, in Christian doctrine one of the Three Kings who visited the newborn Christ, is said to have been Emperor of the Orient. His gift was frankincense, an aromatic oil that symbolized prayer. Saint Gaspar's feast day is January 6.

He went out to the pantry and cut a few sausages from the hook, then tucked in the bed sheets and took off his pajamas, which were yellowed around the neck. He spent the afternoon making small preparations. Above all, he wanted to devote adequate attention to the box containing his gallstones.

First, he placed it on the television, just to see. After viewing it from several angles, he realized that the color of the box coordinated better with the tapestry in the background. He moved it to the cupboard, right next to the Eiffel Tower and the Diskobolos, a gift from the soccer federation when he had left active service in the club. At first, he thought he had found the perfect spot; but the tea set decorated with Paris-blue plums, which stood deeper in the cabinet, caused him to waver. Since the color of the box tended toward a dirty yellow, the blue plums seemed too bright and detracted from the effect of the porcelain.

He thought about the matter for a while.

Toward evening he made his decision. He cleared everything out of the cabinet—all sorts of national trinkets, a souvenir gondola, an engraved cup containing his father's dentures—and put it all in a drawer. Bojko wanted a clean surface. He measured the exact width of the shelf, opened the cabinet wings, and positioned the box with the gallstones directly in the center. It felt right.

Just then, he heard his sister's voice in the yard.

Here they come, he thought grimly.

Everything became clear to Bojko as soon as his brother-in-law entered, dressed in a military uniform cinched tightly around the waist. Bojko was barely able to mumble, "Gd evng—"

He tried to remain collected. He couldn't let his brother-in-law know he was impressed by the uniform of the Army Reserve. He behaved graciously, served wine and water, and told a few jokes to get the evening off to a good start. When there was no response, he retreated into the corner, across from his brother-in-law and Dodo. They sat beside each other, the son imitating the father—legs crossed, head tilted, clicking his tongue now and then. Neither one seemed inclined to wish him a happy St. Gaspar Day.

At one point, Bojko walked over toward the porcelain box. His brother-in-law sat up straight on the couch, and like his shadow, Dodo did the same. But as soon as Bojko returned to his prior position, the tension subsided. *It's a war of nerves*, Bojko concluded, his gaze fixed on the box.

When his sister finally brought out the tray with his sausages, his brother-in-law and nephew came to the table. Bojko smelled a ripe moment. As fast as his physical condition allowed, he grabbed the box of gallstones with both hands. *It's now or never*, he told himself before turning to his guests.

His brother-in-law's eyes popped out of his head. Bojko had caught him in a semi-seated position, just as he was putting the first bite in his mouth.

After Bojko took off the lid, all hell broke loose. His brother-in-law spat a piece of sausage casing into his hand, then looked around as though in a trance. He stood up abruptly, in a state of agitation. Moving toward the door, he knocked against the table with his thigh, and all the glasses tinkled. Bojko's sister massaged her withered cheeks with her fingers. Dodo's eyes skittered tensely from his father to his uncle.

His brother-in-law had left, and Bojko, standing in the middle of the room, continued to hold the open box of gallstones. All at once, he forgot his wound, his diet, and the lightheadedness that caused his nose to bleed from time to time. Waves of gratification flowed through his body like a breeze caressing his fevered brow, until his sister's voice drew him out of his fogginess.

"You shouldn't have done that to him!" his sister scolded.

Bojko threw on the first thing he found in his closet and went outside. Sitting on the veranda, he realized he had gone a bit overboard in showing off his gallstones. In the dimness of the yard, he made out a tiny point of light from his brother-in-law's cigarette.

A brief shower had moistened the molehills on the grass, and the soles of Bojko's slippers became heavy with the gooey earth. A cat moved furtively at the edge of the yard. Bojko heard the rhythmic sounds of inhaling and exhaling as he moved in behind his brother-in-law.

"Krgrgh," he coughed out in the dark. All he wanted to do now was extinguish all memories of the past week of home rest. *To forgive is human*, he thought to himself, just as his brother-in-law put out his cigarette on the damp ground.

Bojko gasped for breath several times, like a frightened child, then turned his head toward his brother-in-law. This was the closest they'd ever been to each other.

In a complete change of plan, Bojko said, "Don't sin against the soul, but accept what has been dealt to you. Praise God and don't take this seriously. Ah, if only I had such an energetic kid." He continued in the kind of voice one heard in radio dramas.

"A true gift from God; he's going to be smart in school, you'll see," he lied, standing over his brother-in-law. "You've got a wife who loves you, a wife who'd do anything for you." Bojko's voice assumed a steady, friendly tone.

"Just think how many people would kill for what you have. Thank God and appreciate what you have. Don't worry about this."

His brother-in-law's head swung left and right and finally came to rest against his chest, as though the firm cord connecting it to his spine were suddenly severed.

Bojko took hold of his chin and said, "You have everything I want. Yeah, yeah, but hey, I don't have it and that's that. It just didn't work out for me, see? Nobody wants me. They just don't, what can I do? You know, I'd like to have all that, too—a wife, a son like that. A house, a car, a cottage on the coast. But I don't need to tell you this, do I?"

Bojko shook his brother-in-law's listless head. "You hear me?"

He appeared lost, discombobulated, as though Bojko's words weren't getting through.

"So what if you don't have gallstones?" Bojko said in a voice that masked a grim satisfaction. He let go of his brother-in-law's unshaved chin, realizing he'd been a little premature on the subject of the gallstones.

"Okay, now," he soothed, trying to salvage the situation, but his brother-in-law's head had slid down to his chest again.

"No, I don't—" his brother-in-law responded. His shoulders slumped. His hands hung against his thighs like rubber bands. Not even the uniform could improve on the picture he made.

"That's right, you said it—I don't have gallstones!"

"What I meant to say was that you don't have them *yet*, but you will!"

"No, I won't," his brother-in-law said bitterly. "If I haven't gotten them by now, I never will."

Bojko's thoughts returned to his poor sister. "Ah fuck it," he groaned. "You always were a pessimist!"

Then his brother-in-law leaned against the damp trunk of the cherry tree and seemed to pull himself together.

The muscles in Bojko's face began to twitch. His brother-in-law dilated his nostrils then sneezed. Their eyes met.

Bojko asked, "You eat red meat, right?"

"Yes, I do," his brother-in-law said tersely.

"How often?"

"Every meal."

"Are you sure?"

"I never go without it. Ask Kata."

"Have you ever been on a diet?"

His brother-in-law didn't even need to think about that. "No, I haven't."

"So there you go." Bojko's mood brightened. "What are you so teed off about?"

His brother-in-law shrugged his shoulders. He seemed embarrassed by the whole scene.

"Now listen up," Bojko told him. "Next year, when my Name Day comes along again, I'll be coming over, and by then you'll have them, I guarantee you. You can spit right in my face if you don't. Just remember what I told you. Figure on the period right around Three Kings Day. Pick out a nice container, crystal or something like that, you know? Kata's got a lot of pretty boxes around the house."

His brother-in-law gave him a curt smile.

"Czech crystal," Bojko added, giving his brother-in-law, who was still bobbing his head back and forth, a thumbs-up sign. Still leaning against the cherry tree, he gulped down a glob of saliva as his gaze wandered over the neighborhood, the former industrial zone.

"I'm sorry, Bojko."

Bojko waved him off with his hand.

"Sorry, but all this, this insanity, where does it all come from? Who knows?" his brother-in-law coughed. "Everyone I know has been operated on. They've all had gallstones, you know that. I'm sure Kata's blabbed about it to you."

Bojko lowered his gaze sympathetically.

"Jole Krizanovic, that Orsolic from the office, the neighbors, the

Cubelas, Pajic Grizelj, and that painter Mato Japundzic. What can I say? He had them out a few months ago, nine beauts, and two handfuls of pebbles before that. All out of the gall bladder. And then I heard about your attack and operation and thought to myself, *Well, what the hell's wrong with me? Why am I the only one who hasn't had gallstones?*"

"Aw come on," Bojko said consolingly.

"Whenever I go to visit someone, they pull out their precious gallstone container. I just look and nod my head. You understand what I'm saying?"

Bojko looked down at the molehills.

"Naturally it's driving me nuts. Little Dodo is already asking, 'What's wrong with you, Daddy?' And what am I supposed to tell him? Huh?" he asked, not waiting for a response.

Bojko exhaled.

"Am I supposed to tell him his dad's some kind of leaf-eater, or a whadyacallit, vegetarian?"

"No way!" said Bojko, moving back.

"A macrobiotic freak?"

"God forbid!"

"Or a bad provider? Should I tell him that?"

There was an extended pause.

"Or that he's on a continuous fast or something?"

"Wait," Bojko said as a sudden brainstorm came upon him. "The boy knows you were in the war!"

His brother-in-law nervously shook his head, as if he had expected just such a comment.

"Nobody remembers that anymore. It's like it came and it went, like it never even happened," said his brother-in-law, as though in mourning for all those lost years. His fingers began to twitch, but he found the strength for one last dignified stand.

"Bojko, you of all people know the only thing you're left with in the end is your gallstones."

As he spoke, his brother-in-law's face disintegrated, his lower lip protruding over his upper, quivering and twisting in a way that boded ill. He raised his head and closed his eyes. In the faraway distance, a candle rebelled against the darkness. Only then did Bojko realize how close his brother-in-law was to tears.

The Man from Bezdan on the Danube

Some places exude a certain hidden horror, and one of those is Bezdan, a small settlement on the Danube. It's probably completely subjective, in the same way fiction is subjective. The small number of people living there are probably no unhappier than those living in comparable outposts in Oregon or Florida. But two elements distinguish this particular place: the first is the name "Bezdan," which means "a bottomless pit" or "an abyss," and the other is that it is the precise spot where for decades the water level of the Danube, Europe's most powerful river, has been measured. "The Danube at Bezdan" was how radio speakers would refer to it, and I still experience an uneasy tingling feeling whenever I hear its name mentioned. So it's logical that the possessor of secret skills in my story should come from Bezdan, the man wearing the shabby suit from the 1950s, riding on the bicycle with metal panels. And the cats in the story? They are collateral damage and, as such, deserve our everlasting respect.

G.N. ✚

The Man From Bezdan on the Danube

"How did that cat ever manage to finagle its way into this house?"
Vlatko loudly cried out from time to time, directing a dark look
at the rest of the household, searching for any small sign of
comprehension on their faces. Zana just shrugged her shoulders. It
was a difficult question.

Several years had passed since they had taken Skembo under
their care. The neighborhood had been under construction, and
cats had roamed around in packs—tailless, cross-eyed, with noses
that had been carved up by many ferocious claws. At night, cat eyes
glimmered out from nearby building sites which a fleet of bulldozers
had senselessly laid to waste. Some of the pitiful creatures infiltrated
various households—the first generation to experience petting
and regular meals. At first the families fed them leftovers, then
tinned fish and pâté right out of the can. In time they moved on to
Whiskas and fresh liver. These cats were clearly not hooked on milk.

And then Skembo showed up, the first cat in the Silovic family.
Vlatko could not recall when or under what circumstances, but Kico
and Hrvojka, who were very young at the time, had squealed with joy.

One morning they found a large litter in the basement: eight or
maybe nine transparent kittens in a cluster, meowing blindly and
helplessly. The children were beside themselves.

Then came something that Vlatko would never have dreamed
possible. Just as he finished the house he had tirelessly slaved over
for years—brick by brick, from foundation to roof, eleven years of

hard labor, skimping, and sacrifice—he was diagnosed with diabetes. Every week he had to go to a clinic for insulin injections, which his health insurance paid for. If he let his blood sugar drop, he became tense, so Zana placed chocolate cookies on various surfaces throughout the house.

In the evening, when the kids went to sleep, Vlatko and Zana would tackle their problems. So far they had had no difficulty resolving the burning issues as they arose: the Bavarian wood siding, a car rental, whether Kico should start school at age six, a lawn or landscaping, Limex bicycle, and so on, issue after issue, the pros and the cons. Vlatko would present the issue, clarify it from several angles, and Zana would ask follow-up questions. Sometimes they allowed the issues to ferment for a few days, then they would sit back down at the table, share a beer, and come to a reasonable solution. They enjoyed a clear partnership, in raising their children as well as in making material decisions.

With Skembo's litter they experienced their first parting of the minds. Zana immediately fell back on generally accepted conduct: in such cases, distribute the kittens among all the neighbors. She vaguely recalled that her grandmother had done the same thing. At the same moment, a light went on in Vlatko's head. "That'll never fly—all the other cats in the neighborhood have had large litters as well!"

After a while, Zana was forced to admit the imprudence of her proposal. "If we try to feed them, they'll die out one by one anyway," she realized after a few days, accepting the high mortality rate of kittens. "And then we'll still look good in the children's eyes," she added.

But Vlatko didn't like this suggestion, either.

"Honey, you are a smart cookie, smart enough to know a little something about kittens," he said, then he rattled on about the endless possible scenarios in connection with the nine lives of cats. Actually, several things were turning around in his head. He exhaled, clicked his tongue, tugged on an earlobe. He was distant these days, which Zana attributed to his reaction to insulin.

"Then let's keep them all and whatever happens, happens," Zana proposed heartily one evening. This was after the kittens had begun to appear in the yard, under Skembo's close supervision. The children requested lots of milk for Skembo. Plus fish-flavored Whiskas—Skembo liked that best—as a supplement.

This time Vlatko let out a rude curse in front of Zana. Monthly expenses were constantly increasing in order to satisfy Skembo's needs. The last expense had been huge, about as much as a family with two chain-smokers would spend on cigarettes. The amount would increase as the kittens became cats. Zana was disconcerted.

"And this will be sooner than you think, because kittens grow like weeds," he continued, trying to feed her fears. He mentioned that expenses would continue to rise to cover the damage the cats would cause until they settled into stable behavior patterns.

"They pull on the curtains, chew the carpet, scratch the chairs, tear the wall hangings, and shit all over the place." As he ran down the list, Zana sank deeper and deeper into melancholy. "Need I mention what pleasure they take in pissing on the cellar windowsills?" Vlatko threw out, imbued with sudden courage. "That's like ammonia, it eats up everything, sweetheart."

Zana saw red. "Well, then what do you suggest?" she spat out. This was the first time she had raised her voice since they began their conversations about the kittens.

Vlatko gave her a piercing look: "Have they gone to sleep?" he asked, gesturing upstairs with his head, in the direction of the children's bedrooms.

"Look, honey," he began, touching her hand as though summoning other, more intimate times. "I can just stuff them into the trunk and drop them off near some other village—" He hadn't finished the sentence when Zana, as though suddenly scorched by fire, pulled her hand away from his.

"Wait a minute, I won't take them all at once. The first time it would be, say, five, four, or maybe just three. Why shouldn't I take three at first? Just to see how it works out. The children wouldn't even know they were missing," he said, as though trying to drive a bargain. Zana was shooting hateful looks from across the table.

"It doesn't have to be all at once," he repeated firmly, but Zana had retreated into herself. By the rigid posture she had assumed, he knew she was wounded, and deeply.

Skembo's litter made excellent progress. By summer, the kittens had grown much larger. In this first period, they were all known as Skembies. Kico and Hrvojka hadn't wanted to give them names until their genders became evident, because they didn't want to repeat the mistake they had made with Skembo, thinking she was a tomcat and giving her a full-blooded masculine name. Vlatko found the first cat shit on the dining room cupboard. *No wonder people say someone stinks like cat shit*, he thought to himself. He called Zana so she could see what awaited her.

"Multiply that by the number of kittens, and what you get is a house full of cat shit," he warned her, but his wife continued silently sweeping the floor.

The time soon came when the family had to watch where they stepped. The kittens seemed to appear out of nowhere, getting tangled in someone's legs, insisting on being petted, and suddenly jumping into someone's lap. Vlatko had no idea cats could make so much noise! The formerly pregnant Skembo had to be fed extra so she would have enough milk. The children paid close attention, ensuring that no meals were missed. Once a day, the daughter, Hrvojka, would count the kittens and gauge their weight by holding each in the palm of her hand.

Discussion about the kittens' fate had somehow begun to wane. Vlatko was miserable at how fast they grew. Once in a while he would take out his anger on one of the kittens. Pretending to pet it, he would baby-talk loudly for all to hear, "pwetty widdo koody kiddy," and then carry it off to some hidden corner—far from the family—where he could cuff it undisturbed. He hoped to drive them out of the house. But what was a slap here and there compared to all the love and affection to be had from the other members of the household? Nothing at all.

Summer passed, and the cat family was still a complete unit. Meanwhile the children discovered that cats loved innards, hot dogs, and salami. And it all had to be fresh.

Ajo Jajic from Bezdan on the Danube appeared at the Silovics' unannounced. He was going from house to house on a black bicycle, offering his services for early spring cultivation projects. He wore a formal-style jacket from the 1950s, a mousy color with a plaid pattern, and his pantcuffs were rolled up, probably because of the digging. A collapsible shovel bounced against his hip. His short-brimmed hat was tipped down toward his face. His hourly fee was so low that Vlatko couldn't refuse.

Ajo Jajic was a consummate shoveler, his technique perfect, and he didn't even take off his jacket. By evening, he had asked for water only twice. When he finished, Vlatko took him a beer. They sat down on the freshly dug earth and turned toward the house, where squirming cats could be seen in every window. The subject came up all by itself.

Vlatko felt sorry for himself and opened up his heart. Besides, the guy in the jacket could have been his father, or at least an older brother. He went back into the house for more beer. It felt good to spend time with someone who was willing to listen to his troubles. Night had already fallen when the close-mouthed fellow from Bezdan on the Danube asked Vlatko if he wanted to see a trick.

At first, Vlatko was suspicious, but he finally agreed to take Ajo into the cellar, among the cats. Ajo pulled a regular nylon bag from his pocket, blew into it, shook it, then spread it open.

"Go on, throw one in!" he said.

Vlatko hesitated.

"Come on, come on," Ajo urged him, holding the bag open. "Just one!"

Vlatko arbitrarily grabbed the closest kitten. He threw it in, and Ajo shot him a pinched look.

"First you stretch out the sack, good and tight, as though you want to rip it apart—" Vlatko had become interested in all this. He was closely following the squirming cat in the sack.

"Then you tie the ends of the sack together, one over the other!"

"Aha," Vlatko blinked in the dim light of the cellar, holding his breath. The old guy's hands, the color of clay, performed the operation in a brusque, intuitive manner, using a series of simple movements. For the final move, Ajo from Bezdan on the Danube paused for a moment so that Vlatko could take hold of the ends.

"You make a bow, and then another," said the man from Bezdan, "and then you pull all at once from both ends." He did this skillfully. The bag deflated, and after a few moments, the whimpering inside came to an end.

"In a split second, she's finished," he explained.

Vlatko never again saw Ajo Jajic in the neighborhood, but he adopted his method. He told Zana and the children the kitten had probably been run over by a car.

"You yourselves know how crazily people drive nowadays," he

said, attempting to prepare them for the next loss. By the end of the month, he had taken care of almost all the cats. The biggest problem he had was with Skembo herself, who refused to go into the sack. He had to act silently at night when everyone else was in bed, which caused him endless frustration. When he finally succeeded in luring her into the sack with some pâté and tied the bow the way Ajo had taught him, her sharp claws managed to penetrate the sack, scratching his hand.

Now only one kitten remained, the one he presumed was a tomcat. Several months later this proved to be a gross error. The only surviving Skembie showed up with a tummy, just like her mother. A day or two later she gave birth to eight or nine kittens. Of course Vlatko knew what had to be done.

Vlatko vacillated at first on the strangling schedule. First he had wanted to get rid of them all at once. He got a bit carried away and finished off half of them in the first few days.

The children had become extremely ill-tempered, and Zana had shown suspicion for the first time. One evening, after they had split a beer, she started on the subject Vlatko had been dreading.

"Only three or four cars go down our street every day, and in just three days, six kittens have disappeared. Is it possible that every car that passed by ran over a kitten?" She spoke in as poised a voice as she could muster.

Vlatko played the fool. "I was wondering that same thing myself," he said.

Zana directed a sharp, questioning look at the scratches on his hands. He realized he had to slow down.

Hrvojka and Kico set up guardposts along the road and manned them in shifts. Vlatko only chuckled to himself, knowing that school would start soon and the children would have to relax their vigil. And so it was. The first week of school he managed to get rid of one more kitten. He had a strong alibi, because a bulldozer had been working on a lot in the neighborhood.

"And the bodies? Where are the bodies?" the children wailed, in tears. Vlatko explained that he had wanted to spare them the horrible sight.

Then came another unexpected shock. Before he knew it, there was a third generation of Skembies. Vlatko's blood sugar went sky high, and he had to increase his insulin dose. For the first time in years he took refuge in the local bar. Alcohol got the best of him, and he found himself telling a neighbor about the sack trick. The neighbor asked him to come over and give him a hand. He had two litters he didn't know what to do with. Vlatko solved his problem that same night with a single sack.

Soon others arrived, requesting the same favor. Some even offered to pay, but it seemed inappropriate to Vlatko to make money from such a service. He simply considered it a neighborly gesture. Generally, he would go into someone's basement with a bag in his pocket and there, surrounded by a chorus of meows, perform—in ever quicker fashion—the duty he had come to execute.

After he finished, the people would buy him a drink. He never stayed too long, especially since the host's children always seemed to be looking at him suspiciously. He would have a coffee without sugar, sometimes a Diet Coke, and exchange a few words with the neighbor. He never mentioned the cats. Before setting off for home, he asked to use the restroom so that he could rub some lotion on his hands, to ease the scratches. Then he would hear the cry of a child from somewhere in the house. "Strangler!" they sometimes yelled, in hoarse, muffled voices. He was confident the parents would deliver appropriate punishment to children who behaved so rudely.

The fourth—or was it the fifth?—generation of Skembies was meeting its end; this litter was predominantly black and promised large and hearty offspring. But at the end of a new strangulation cycle, Vlatko was confronted with the same dilemma he had tried to resolve at the time of the first litter: which kittens were tomcats, and which should be spared?

In the half-dark cellar, he poked around in vain at the kittens' intimate parts. He failed to determine the gender. Then came the night he knew was destined to arrive: the night he lost control. Swaying back and forth, no doubt due to increased blood sugar, he went all the way in a dusty basement, in the darkness and the silence, broken only by the meowing and whining. The bag was filled and emptied several times, but it didn't pop, which was most important to him at that moment. Vlatko was gasping, bloodied around the ankles, and the meowing grated on his ears. Besides that, his neck was stiff from the intimate organ inspections. He plugged away to the last kitten in the litter.

At dawn, still feeling the effects of the previous night, he gathered all his fishing poles from the garage. He had his needles and insulin ready in a small pouch. As he drove around aimlessly, he was overcome with a desire to be out in nature.

The sun had already come up by the time he got to Bezdan. The Danube was powerful there, wide. The only sound to be heard was the monotonous croaking of frogs. He descended the bank to the shore and got his line where he wanted it on the first cast, outside the current. He attached small bells to the tops of the other poles, silenced them with his hands, stuck them into the ground, and sat down on a box. He attached a fly to a piece of stretched line. Flowers were blooming along the riverbank. He inhaled deeply, and his mood became lighter. A pleasant breeze lulled him to sleep. The Danube quietly flowed toward the sea.

Small beads of sweat had just begun to form on his upper lip when the tinkling of bells awakened him. Vlatko moved quickly to the pole, but it wasn't bent, and the fly was still on the end of the line. The sun disappeared for a moment, then one by one, the frogs leapt into the water. Silence descended.

A dark figure at the river drew Vlatko's attention. He watched closely as a bicyclist slowly emerged from the shadow of the underbrush. The sun was harsh, beating down from the sky and reflecting off the water. Vlatko shielded his eyes with his hand. The man on the bicycle was pedaling downhill into the water, breaking the surface and going silently downward. Shimmering out from the rear wheel was a thin trail of water that quickly dispersed and disappeared.

When the man reached Vlatko's eye level, he took off his short-brimmed hat. From the muddy banks where he stood, Vlatko recognized Ajo, old Ajo Jajic from Bezdan on the Danube. With one hand he guided the handlebars of the black bicycle, and with the other he waved to Vlatko, making wide circles with his hat. Vlatko noticed the plaid suit, slightly tailored, but wide through the shoulders and around the neck. One of the man's pantlegs was held up by a clothespin.

He kept on waving. For a moment Vlatko raised his hand, as though to give a final greeting to the old man, but he quickly reconsidered. Ajo opened his mouth, and Vlatko stared as the mute, toothless jaw gaped open, and the hat continued its revolutions. At the same tempo, the bicycle went down, down—below the surface of the water.

At the point where the Danube made its final twist before flowing comfortably on and merging with the setting sun, Ajo became a small spot in the middle of the river. Before he completely disappeared, the reflector on the bicycle's rear fender, the type referred to as a cat's eye, caught a ray of sun, which glittered diabolically before the river regained its calm.

The Barefoot Temptation

The people running the country I live in often emphasize the fact that Croatia, along with Poland, the late Pope John Paul II's country of birth, is the most Catholic country in Europe. They are probably right about that. Forty-five years of official atheism left scarcely a trace on our nation; the large population of former atheists has almost completely died out. Wherever you turn, there are new churches, religious processions, and, in the media, priests with the status of pop stars. I admit this all caught me a bit unprepared. In 1999, a skinny guy in a white shirt and narrow, old-fashioned black tie suddenly appeared and laid siege to my house. I listened courteously to him as he warned me, in a private session, that the sins of mankind were leading us to a final Judgment Day. He misconstrued my courtesy for a desire to join the Jehovah's Witnesses. Although he had wasted his time with me, I hadn't wasted mine with him. Our session resulted in the story "The Barefoot Temptation."

G.N. ✚

the
survival
league

The Barefoot Temptation

Actually, it all began with a dream. Vjeko later described his experience as a surge of energy pumping into his body—a quiet, dreamy infusion.

That morning he felt like wearing something special, something clean, white, yielding. He shaved off his sparse beard with his father's razor, then made a perfect part in his hair, slicking it down with walnut oil. He sauntered into the kitchen with a smile that would henceforth be a permanent fixture on his face and whispered what had just transpired to his mother. As she grated onions, Jaca regarded him from behind her frizzy bangs, a little taken aback by the perfect part. Just as she began to say something, he raised both hands and, imitating the sonorous voices of the ancient prophets, said: "We hear them speak in our languages about God's great gifts!"

Meanwhile, Jaca routinely turned on the fan above the oven.

"Apostles two: eleven," Vjeko added.

Unlike her husband, Jaca had always shown sympathy for the inclinations of her only son. She and Vjeko had always shared secrets with each other. Jole came home from work at 3:10 PM and immediately after lunch would return to the construction site, exhausted and suffering from indigestion. Everyone knew Jole was swamped with work in the summertime. Builders took advantage of the warm weather, and renovation projects were in full swing. Jole had no idea what was happening at home, and he knew even less about what had happened prior to the night Vjeko described as the turning point in his life. "Ah, if it had only been winter when all the projects were shut down," Jole and Jaca said later, sighing. Bad weather allowed Jole to leave the office and drop by the house whenever he wanted.

"Maybe together we could have recognized the signs earlier and reacted in time," the two of them said.

But God doesn't choose his seasons.

Jaca swore that nothing had seemed suspicious. She often saw the boys Vjeko spent time with in his room. They were nice boys—Jaca particularly emphasized their good manners—Vjeko's age, between twenty and twenty-five, hair parted on the right, and dressed in pleated suit pants into which they tucked their crisp-collared, starched shirts. There was something old-fashioned in their manner, which Jaca saw as a commendable sense of propriety. She lined up their shoes neatly in the foyer. They didn't smoke in the room or leave crumbs.

"Well! Any mother would be happy to have any of them as a son-in-law!" Jaca said to her husband later, justifying her behavior.

The boys would talk quietly for hours. Jaca would hear monotone voices behind the locked door. It seemed to her that her son was just listening and paying attention, which did not surprise her at all. Sometimes she served them elderberry juice and salty snacks on the tray engraved with images of deer.

"Guests are sacred to me!" she said later in her own defense when her husband accused her of being naïve.

At that time, Jole was occupied from early in the morning, dealing with problems on the job. After all, everything depended on him, the owner and director. He went from site to site, clambering up wobbly ladders to give a tongue-lashing to a sunburned worker who was sloughing off, or yelling over the racket to the crane operators that they'd be looking for other employment if they didn't shape up. From the wholesalers to the carpenters, he vaguely suspected everyone of stealing from him.

"They're all a bunch of sons of bitches you have to keep your eye on all the time!" he would say to his wife to explain away his constant absence.

When somebody told him, during one of his quick stops at a site, that his son looked impressive in a suit, a real man's man, Jole detected no sarcasm. He scoffed and responded in his usual way after all these years on the construction site.

"Ha? Him in a suit?" he blustered. "That snot-nosed kid doesn't even know how to knot a tie!"

At this he laughed uncontrollably, while his employees dispersed throughout the site, eyes averted. But Jole wasn't crazy, and he wasn't naïve like his wife. By the end of the day he had squeezed the truth from his secretary.

With as much tact as possible, she told him what people in the company were saying: "That your son is a Jehovah's witness." She forced this out, watching fearfully as the director's nostrils flared.

People who are always out in the field, always covered with dust and working under deadlines—these people want things at home to function; they want order, a basic rhythm, and at least a little gratitude for the comforts they offer their loved ones. Jole had big plans for his son. He needed someone he could trust, someone he could train for the job, who, when the right time came, could take over his cash cow. He was thinking of all this as he drove his jeep home, shattered by the news. As he was stopped at a red light at one of the corners in the busiest part of the city, where the pedestrian zone feeds into one of the main arteries, he saw a face he would recognize among a thousand others.

People behind Jole were honking and flashing their lights. He was clogging up traffic, but he found it difficult to turn away from the sight of Vjeko offering passersby a fistful of illustrated color leaflets. He recognized the suit his son was wearing as one of his own, an old suit he thought his wife had given away long ago to some shelter for the poor.

And that part in Vjeko's hair! First Jole's jaws locked up, then, suddenly seized by panic, he sank deeply into his seat.

Did anyone see me? It was as though his skittering eyes were asking this question. *Maybe some envious competitor who can hardly wait to ruin my reputation in the field?*

Take it easy, calm down, he repeated to himself as he inhaled deeply, attempting to regain self-control. Although the day was overcast, he lowered the sun visors and crept into the first side street without even signaling. His heart was pounding. What he needed now was some isolated, backstreet café and a strong drink.

Jole was late for lunch, but his family hadn't wanted to start without him. A bit drunk, he made a wide berth around his wife and, keeping his hands in his pockets, got into his son's face.

Vjeko kept his composure. "Let's say grace," he said, palms pressed together above his soup bowl.

"We give thanks to Him for this wonderful meal," Vjeko said quietly, suffering under the burden of his father's breath.

Jole looked in surprise at Jaca, who had promptly acknowledged her son's murmurings. Jaca, following her son's hand movements, crossed herself. At this moment, Jole's huge fingers headed toward his son's throat, but halfway there, his hand began to cramp painfully. The saliva in Vjeko's cleanly shaven mouth formed knots that traveled fitfully down his throat like peas in a constricted pod, carrying away all the color in his face.

A spoon fell off the edge of one of the plates, the glasses began to clink, and the surface of the soup started to bubble.

"Jehovah's eyes are on the righteous, his eyes administering to their prayers," Vjeko proclaimed finally, as his gaze traveled over his father, from head to toe.

Then, emboldened, he added: "First Peter three: twelve."

Vjeko made quick progress. His good memory and the work habits he had gained in school helped him to master the learning materials. On rainy days he would stay in his room, surrounded by practical literature. But on the first clear day he would rush out, his hair always impeccably parted. He clutched a black bag that was packed with brochures. His posture was erect; his face was open to the world.

Jaca barely found the time to iron all his shirts and the pleats on his pants, but she couldn't refuse his request for cleanliness. He had thrown away his jeans and tennis shoes; T-shirts he had brought in by the truckload from Trieste and other far-flung places were donated to the Red Cross. Jaca secretly liked Vjeko's new image. But sometimes, as she shook dandruff from his jacket, she called attention to various details of modern tailoring.

"Not even Christ was self-indulgent," Vjeko would remind her.

He was capable of standing all day in the square, calm and dignified, offering leaflets and brochures in a manner many of his fellow respectable citizens admired. Soon Vjeko became one of a three-member group that went from house to house and apartment to apartment. His perseverance served him well in this new task. He conducted conversations on doorsteps, even from sidewalks, trying to speak over the barking of dogs that had been sicced on him or the revving of engines inside garages. He was not discouraged by the doors slammed in his face or by the sudden silences that came after the homeowner looked through the peephole to see who it was.

"Good news has to find its way to them," he would tell his listless colleagues.

In time, he won over many apartments, and sometimes, at an entrance to a building, an entire group of people would stop and listen. He captured their attention with his clever views and the boundless energy he invested in his conversation. Sometimes his mouth would become dry, lacking even a drop of saliva. He would proudly reject a glass of juice, even on those days when his raspy voice cut his sentences in half. He had seen through alcohol long ago, and he wasn't interested in coffee.

"Do not love the world or what is in it," he instructed. "Whosoever loves the world holds no love for Him!"

Vjeko would come home late, pale and hoarse, but the night lamp at his work table continued to burn well into the night. Jole, a few meters away on the other side of the wall, tried unsuccessfully to fall asleep.

Weeks passed, and the clear weather suited for outdoor projects was gradually replaced by rain. The first frost arrived, there was less work, and Jole had a substantial amount of time for contemplation.

"Talk to him," Jaca would urge him.

So Jole would burst into his son's room then—confronted with what he found there—rush out again, slam the door, and loudly lower all the blinds in the house. Then he would retreat to the room they called the winter garden, aglow with artificial sunlight. Those days he complained of the strange transparency of his veins.

"Old age," Jaca would tell him comfortingly.

Early in the morning, Jole, now plagued by insomnia, would roam about the house. He would hear Vjeko putting on his shoes and quietly tiptoeing across the floor. He would try to summon an earlier closeness by gently squeezing his son's shoulder. The pale light of the winter morning would briefly reveal their exchange of glances, until a sudden thought would upset Jole's stomach.

"For God's sake, at least change your locations a little," he would suggest.

Vjeko would carefully retreat toward the outside door. Since the
day he had experienced his father's rough fingers moving toward
his throat, he realized his earthly mission would be subject to
uncontrolled reactions from his nearest and dearest.

"As long as you're standing on the street," Jole would continue
in a phlegmy voice, "then at least change positions. Move around a
little! People don't have to see you every day on the same corner,"
he would say, barely moving his lips. In the early dawn, dead tired,
he would yell after his son, "And don't you dare ring our relatives'
doorbells!"

That's how Vjeko's day would begin. But his joy about spreading
the truth of the heavenly kingdom would quickly disperse the
clouds he carried from the house into the streets. New challenges
awaited him, and sometimes he barely endured till sunset; every day
he became more inspired in his presentation and more committed to
the tasks entrusted to him.

News about Vjeko's skill in disseminating the good word spread
through the small community. He decided to specialize in his
work and direct his efforts toward eradicating superstition, which
had become prevalent in Christian households. He began to focus
his family visits on only the most endangered of souls, those who
needed him most.

"Jesus drove out demons, and his students did the same." Vjeko
would begin his day's work with these words. He would move
from example to example, using quotes from the Bible to illustrate
concrete cases, delivering a tirade right on the spot about the deadly
repercussions of trifling with evil spirits. He rushed to his point with
his rich vocabulary and exalted bearing.

"Awaken!" he thundered. "Their goal is to deter us from the only
hope for mankind!"

His mobile phone made him available night and day for
those who yearned for his words. He would travel to the farthest
peripheries to make calls: to settlements without street names or
house numbers, to places where his distended black bag attracted
the attention of incorrigible lawbreakers. He had been robbed twice,
but upon opening the bag the attackers were disappointed with the
plunder and took out their rage on Vjeko's frail body. He persevered
and never asked for days off to recover.

"Jehovah's Angels stand over those who fear him, and they are delivered." He would continue where he had left off the day before. He felt the energy accumulated within him restore itself daily; then it simply flowed out into the community.

The first concrete results were soon visible. He broke up a fortune-telling ring in a nursing home and persuaded a mother to forego an abortion and carry her baby to term despite the projected due date of Friday the 13th. He never regretted using his precious time to explain to a demoralized housepainter that walking under a ladder was no reason to despair or quit his job. He went to houses where loved ones had died and closed the windows.

"The soul will find a way to reach God," he told the grieving families.

Even the sense of lassitude that comes with spring did not faze him. Though pale and transparent, Vjeko plunged into in a host of activities. He never complained of pains. He slept very little, but his face exuded freshness. It was important to him to expand the circle of those he had enlightened as widely as possible. When one of his colleagues would ask him in confidence about his methods, Vjeko's answer was always the same: "love and faith."

One morning he remained fixed in prayer longer than usual. The day was already well along, but Vjeko, kneeling on the linoleum floor, was preparing himself for the task he considered most difficult thus far in his short but successful career. He realized he could no longer fool himself or his loved ones. Doubts swirled around in his head.

"Am I as hypocritical as the Pharisees?" he asked himself. "The Son of God also started with those closest to him. Can I be a worthy disciple," he whispered, "if my own flesh and blood don't believe in me?"

The one thing he had been trying to escape had finally caught him.

From the kitchen, Jaca saw Vjeko moving along the hall. Then she heard him enter their bedroom, open the closets, the armoires, and the large dresser drawer. She caught him with his hands up to the elbows in his father's undergarments.

"Mama," he asked, "doesn't he have a single pair of socks?"

For the first time since Vjeko had been enlightened by faith, Jaca felt a clear twinge of unease. She approached Vjeko and pointedly closed everything he had opened. Then she set herself, a live barrier, between her son and her husband's underwear.

"No, there isn't a single pair," she answered brusquely.

Vjeko's silence at that moment could only be seen as a bad thing.

All afternoon, Jaca tried to focus on her cooking, but Vjeko always seemed to be at her heels. An otherwise simple roux burst into flames. The beans refused to cook all the way through. Tasting them, Jaca realized she had oversalted. She almost threw out the smoked meat with the bean husks.

All of a sudden, she felt overwhelmed. She stood and squinted, holding on to the edge of one of her kitchen appliances.

"You'll feel better if you tell me everything, believe me," Vjeko said, breathing down her neck.

"Like Jesus, we look only for the good in people," he whispered, pushing her tense shoulders downward.

Jaca sat down in a chair. Her gold caps gleamed from the corners of her mouth, one after the other as her mouth widened, like a traffic signal. Something shattered inside her. Her shoulders relaxed and drooped, together with the thin lines of her mouth.

"Yes, it's true that he hasn't worn socks for three years now," she began in a raised tone, as though wrenching the words from a constriction deep inside her. "He gave them up the summer I talked him into taking the mudbaths. That was the first time your father had had a vacation in thirty years," she said with the obligatory respect.

Vjeko shot out of his chair and approached his mother. His hands, pressed together, rested under his chin. He listened obsessively, nodding his head slightly from time to time. He had already mastered the art of being a patient confessor.

"He became very weak there in the baths, from the sulfur. Oh Lord, how it burned one's eyes!" Jaca recalled. "And he, you know how he is, all he could think about was work, and his mobile phone was ringing non-stop, all bad news from the construction site.

"Then, all of a sudden, he told me he was going to take a look around, breathe in the fresh air, you know. He was gone a long time, and when he came back to the pool, he was distracted, troubled." Jaca's account became increasingly fluid.

"I was suspicious—why lie about it?—since he'd been gone a long time," she said, as though justifying her doubts. "And when I pressed him about it, he admitted he'd just come back from the woman who gazes into the crystal ball. You'd know better what that's called."

"Hmmm. Fortune-telling," Vjeko mumbled, running his tongue over his lips.

"That's it! The poor guy thought at first it was some kind of tourist attraction. It was a woman with a green turban, and in front of her, on a collapsible chair, there was a crystal ball, like in the amusement park. I mean, you pay, and she tells you something, some story. During the session, your father realized this was serious and had nothing to do with tourism or entertainment. But by then it was too late to quit."

"So what did she foretell?" Vjeko asked bitterly.

Jaca's expression suddenly became hollow. The years of security she had found in her kitchen abandoned her. The hanging cupboards, the chopping boards, the steam, the odors, the whirring of the kitchen appliances—all the things in which she had found refuge seemed suddenly endangered, vulnerable.

"She told him he was going to die in his socks," she said quietly.

"And the heavens opened up!" Vjeko interjected and looked up toward the ceiling, which was moist from the steam. "And he took that seriously?"

"She prescribed monthly check-ups. They call it individual treatment."

He jumped to his feet as though stung. He took one step, two, then stopped, turned, and pointed his finger at her: "Jehovah loves the truth and will not abandon those who are loyal to him!" he growled.

Jaca managed to grab hold of his hand.

"He told me not to say anything about it to anybody," she said beseechingly. "He hides it from people," she whimpered, stroking his palms.

Vjeko pushed her away, but gently, not roughly. Working with people he had learned professional responsibility. He believed a dose of mercilessness was required to reach the essence of truth. God's order suffered no exceptions.

He felt the tip of his chin trembling for a while longer before regaining complete control over himself. After returning to his room, he was again the old Vjeko, assured and self-confident. He ignored the knocking at his door and the entreaties. Night found him on his knees, next to the bed. This isolation would be considered a luxury under other circumstances. He remained as motionless as possible, the better to focus on the problem. A breeze through the open window filled his lungs with scents of the night.

It was long past midnight when Vjeko shifted the position of his tingling legs, though he had decided on shock therapy some time ago. It was clear to him that his vacillation had roots in the past. But everything was still so fresh and new, the images still indescribably powerful. A million malicious eyes were watching for any false move. From time to time he felt icy fingers searching for a porous spot on the outer precipices of his soul. They tormented him until the break of dawn.

"Might as well get it over with," he said, exhaling deeply. He took out of his dresser drawer a pair of white sports socks with diagonal stripes that hit a grownup just at the ankle. "Socklets," Jaca called them. They were soft and a little worn out from being washed so often. He placed them over his left palm as though he were about to leave, then turned once again to the wall crucifix. His murmurings were still vibrating on his lips as he considered whether he ought to add something, at least in those few moments of indecision, when he was still trying to figure things out in his mind. And then he crept into the bedroom.

Because his father was a light sleeper, he had decided to keep everything to a minimum—to open the door as little as possible and spend as little time in the room as he could. He had stuffed both socks halfway into his pockets—the left sock in the left pocket, the right in the right. Two steps brought him to his parents' bed. He knew that Jole slept on the window side of the bed. As usual, he was on his back, snoring lightly. His mother emitted no sounds whatsoever. Vjeko lost a split second observing their faces: pale and calm, almost youthful. His father's heels were cold. *Eh, so many winters without socks*, he thought.

He needed three movements for each foot: toes, heels, ankles. Altogether, six coordinated moves. A big toe peeked out of one of the socks, but Jole's face remained peaceful. Clouds raced across the sky.

Vjeko left the room, kissed the cross above his bed, and lay down.

By the time his mother's voice intruded on his consciousness, sleep still had not succeeded in calming his swirling thoughts. She lurched in through the door.

"Heart attack!" she said brusquely. "In his sleep. He didn't suffer."

Vjeko rose up in bed, his phantasms dissipating in the quivering morning light that bathed the room. The first roosters were warming up their drowsy throats. Vjeko shot out of bed and went straight to the bedroom. Holding his breath, he crept over to his father, who was snoring, wheezing, you name it.

"Thank God!" He crossed himself, standing over his father, and skillfully pulled the socks off his feet. This was pretty much the end of Vjeko's career.

With All His Strength

I've never been much of a hiker, but as a skier, I have often had an uneasy feeling as I've contemplated the snowy peaks of a winter night, that feeling of powerlessness the moment you lose the bearings under your feet. In this story I've attempted to describe, in these very specific conditions, the raw fear, as well as the tenderness that can transcend and overcome it. A true event served as a basis for the story, though this is not a necessary precondition to creating the atmosphere, which is the story's most important part. Successfully or not, I transported myself into the minds of people who find themselves dislodged from their everyday complacency and routine and desperately try, with all their strength, to discover the way back.

G.N. ✚

With All His Strength

Right before the main ascent, Bingula pulled off the road into a
bus stop, driving carefully so as not to damage the tires. He left
the motor running in neutral and then, as though apologizing for
something, touched Ivkica's thigh; only then did he get out of the
car. As was his routine, he put snow chains only on the front traction
tires. Before returning to the warmth of the car, he looked upward:
the tips of the snow-laden pine trees sparkled with ice.

But he couldn't get his next-door neighbors, the Sablics, off his
mind. He was plagued by the thought that he hadn't told them he was
going to be away for the weekend. While taking a particularly tricky
curve, he shuddered involuntarily at the image of the Sablics circling
his house, tapping on the shuttered windows, asking themselves where
in God's name Bingula could have disappeared to. A few moments
later, on a straight stretch, he reached again for Ivkica's thigh. He felt
vaguely guilty that they'd exchanged only a few words the entire way.

When they arrived at the mountain lodge, Ivkica said something
about a walk in the fresh air. Bingula gave a nod that was, in his
view, as indefinite as the desire she'd expressed.

They settled into their room in the loft. Ivkica marveled for a
moment at a piece of stonework just under a diagonal window on
the roof.

"Just like on a postcard!" she said, as she pulled wool socks over
her pantyhose.

Bingula agreed, but absently. He was still dwelling on the Sablics,
the next-door neighbors. Maybe it would be best, he thought, to call
them right away and tell them where he was, so they wouldn't worry.

Besides, he didn't need to tell them he was with Ivkica. But what if Mr. Sablic answered the phone? The first thing he'd ask would be, "Is the young lady with you?" Should he lie to him? He could picture how Sablic's nose would flatten as he smirked nastily.

He stared at himself in the bathroom mirror. The stupidity of what he had just done suddenly dawned on him. What on earth would the neighbors think? Especially Mrs. Sablic, who, Bingula thought, might go so far as to call the police. He hesitated in the foyer of their suite. What in the hell was he thinking, just leaving like that?

"Should I take them off or not?" he asked Ivkica, pointing to his boots.

"Aren't we going for a walk?" she sputtered, blinking at him in surprise, in a way that often got on Bingula's nerves.

He considered it unnecessary to become exasperated—especially on issues they could readily agree on.

He went over to her and took her hand, but Ivkica moved away toward the door.

"Let's at least get something to eat first," he called after her, but in vain.

He left the door key with the receptionist, who broke off his telephone conversation and turned to Bingula.

"Mr. Svizac?" he asked brightly.

"Svirac," Bingula corrected him.

"My apologies, Mr. Svirac. Here you are. Number 37."

The massive, dark-hued chandeliers above their heads captured the ambience of the gloomy mountain afternoon. The foyer, with a sculpture in its center, was deserted. Icy air penetrated through a crack between the glass entrance doors. All in all, the lodge didn't seem to be doing well.

Bingula noticed a telephone and immediately began thinking about whether he ought to call the Sablics. Since his wife had passed away, not a single holiday had passed without Mrs. Sablic bringing him a plate of pastries. *If I'd at least left a note or a sign of some kind*, he thought uneasily.

Just then he heard Ivkica doggedly pulling on the entrance door, even though it said "Push." She was one of those people who did the opposite of whatever was written above the door handle.

Bingula went over and roughly pushed the doors outwards, which earned him an insulted look from Ivkica. She seemed about ready to tell him where to go. But just then a freezing gust of wind took away her breath and filled her eyes with tears. She ran down the stairs. Bingula started to warn her about the ice, but reconsidered. If there was one thing he couldn't tolerate, it was a sulking woman.

She went first, setting out on a narrow path, though there were wider, better-traveled ones. Soon they came upon the back pavilion of the lodge, shining with the last traces of the winter sun. They realized they had been going in a circle. Ivkica turned to Bingula, who tried to suppress a smile. She shrugged then turned quickly onto a little path that led down to a narrow valley.

Bingula felt cranky about going downhill, knowing they'd have to climb uphill on the way back, but he followed after her anyway. Although he was warmed up, he was determined not to let his gaze rest more than a second on anything he saw along the way, as though he could not allow the beauty of the landscape to captivate him. He simply had no desire to admire Mother Nature.

But he would call the Sablics for sure, he vowed, as soon as he got back to the lodge. He would tell them where he was, with whom, and why. It had to be done, even at the cost of rupturing relations with his next-door neighbors. *So what if they don't think Ivkica is right for me? That's their problem*, Bingula concluded, feeling suddenly less burdened.

He puffed up his chest and shoved his cold hands deeper into his pockets. He was the type who couldn't stand gloves. In his opinion, gloves were for sissies, like those caps with balls on top or, say, galoshes—he especially hated galoshes on men. He liked to pat himself on the back because in all his fifty-two years, he'd never put on a pair of long underwear—and he never would, he always added, as long as God blessed him with good health.

Thick pines obscured the sky in the clearing the path had led them to. Suddenly a vicious wind came up, delivering three or four strong gusts. They bent over, heads sunk toward their chests, and when they looked up again, their hair was white with frost. Bingula tried to embrace Ivkica, but she deftly squirmed away.

"Should we go back?" he asked, not wanting to sound aggressive. Instead of answering, Ivkica gestured toward a barren mountaintop where two skiers were resting. She pulled her knit cap down over her ears and blinked at Bingula.

As he looked her over for the umpteenth time, Bingula couldn't help thinking what a good catch she was. Those tight buttocks, just like a young girl's—they really got him going. Though Bingula thought of himself as a realistic, mature person, that didn't mean he lacked passion. On the contrary, the realism he had stored away deep within him reassured him that he was on the right path.

He was going to propose to Ivkica. Maybe even in the spring. *When it warms up*, he thought, as he watched her nimbly ascending the hill.

As he fumbled for a cigarette in his jacket, it occurred to him that if Ivkica had been living an immoral life, as the Sablics contended, the county court wouldn't have accepted her as a juror. This thought comforted him.

He contemplated the weekend before them. They would enjoy each other's company, alone for three days, without the Sablics breathing down their necks. As far as Bingula was concerned, they didn't even need to leave the room. They could be naked under the covers with a bottle of champagne nearby.

When they reached the mountaintop, the skiers were already gone. Here at the top, Bingula felt an unpleasant sensation at the back of his head. One of his legs sank into deep snow. He searched for the skiers' silhouettes in the distance. "So, should we head back?" he repeated.

Turning around, he saw Ivkica lying in the snow. He held his hand out to her. She tried to pull him down toward her, but Bingula wouldn't allow himself to be led. He succeeded in getting her back on her feet. Hearing her short breaths—she was breathing through her mouth—he fantasized about her loins, aflame beneath the tights. But just as he bent to kiss her, the wind came up again. The ancient firs rising high above them moaned loudly, and the air was flooded with gray particles of snow.

Thank God, thought Bingula. *Thank God, it's downhill all the way home.*

In the valley, however, they didn't come upon anything remotely resembling the lodge. Finally he held up his hand.

"Let's rest for a minute," he said. Ivkica took his right palm and placed it between her damp wool mittens. A pleasant electrical surge coursed through his body.

Bingula continued to forge through the trees, but the snow-laden branches beat him back.

The path wound gradually uphill. When they emerged onto flat ground, the path forked. Of course they could continue in the same direction, downhill, into the woods; but they could also go uphill.

Bingula was expending a lot of energy. These mountains were wearing him out. The sky was sprinkled with the first evening stars, but the moon hadn't yet appeared. *And maybe it won't*, Bingula thought to himself. He made his way forward decisively, as though he knew the path. Up ahead, he could hear spasmodic sobbing sounds. *Probably the owls*, Bingula thought. His skin tingled, for the first time.

"Maybe this is the wrong path," Ivkica said in a thin, constricted voice.

Oho! So that's the way it's going to be, Bingula said to himself. *The little woman sees fit to speak only when she's in danger.* He was often bothered by Ivkica's limited conversation, and sometimes he got upset when she showed no interest in chatting with him.

For months he had tried in vain to uncover the source of her silence. Now he recalled what had dawned on him back then: that women with fiery pasts were usually quite garrulous; in fact, they never shut up. With this recollection, a wave of contentment washed over him. He gave Ivkica a fond look, which she returned.

"Where on earth are we, Bingo?" she asked softly.

Soon they came to a meadow illuminated by the starry sky. Bingula stopped, and so did Ivkica. The tableau was drenched in voluptuous moonlight; the wind even died down for a moment. Ivkica gently touched Bingula's cold cheek. It seemed to him that she was looking at him in an entirely new way.

"Sing," she whispered to him. Her warm breath filled him with desire.

"Excuse me?" Bingula managed. Her touch on his cheek was almost like tickling. "What do you mean, sing?"

"Sing, please," Ivkica repeated, close to tears.

"Sing?"

"Please, Bingo!"

He stared at his boots; then he made a movement with his right foot, as though he were writing in the snow.

"Look at Me, You Cheating Woman" was the first song that came to mind. He began to sing. As he struggled for the right note—he hadn't even gotten to the second stanza—Ivkica grabbed him firmly by the arm.

"You're howling like a hyena," she said crossly.

She's right, he thought. Luckily, he already had another song on the tip of his tongue. His voice was finally hitting its stride. He tried to sound as spirited as possible as they beat their way through the woods. Bingula's strong bass persevered, guiding the song to its grand finale.

In the distance, the lights of the lodge were still nowhere to be seen. He sang on relentlessly, without interruption:

> I haven't even reached the age to shave,
> And life's already taken what it gave.

He made a good start, but the last stanza petered out unexpectedly. He was thinking about how long it had been since he'd sung this song—since he'd sung at all, in fact, though he did have a good voice. He'd gotten all sorts of compliments as an altar boy in the church choir. He recalled how they'd said that in the entire district, no other alto voice compared with his. *Since those days, I've hardly had a moment to sing*, Bingula thought. He switched over to "The Extraordinary Boy from Downtown":

> My lips are stained with red,
> But these red lips are not for youuuuuu...

Bah, that's so cheap, he grumbled to himself. Just then he felt sharp, icy pangs in his chest. He coughed, spitting out sticky gobs from his lungs.

At least no one but Ivkica will hear me out here, he thought, and he let go again, with all his strength:

> You don't need to tell me a thing...
> Your past,
> Your name.

He felt Ivkica's frail body trembling. His fingers nestled in her small hand.

> If it would make you feel better,
> Embrace me,
> Embrace me.

His toes were frozen. At this mute moment in time, the most important thing for him was to comfort Ivkica.

He thought he saw a glow in the distance. *Are there fireflies in winter?* Bingula wondered. *Not likely.* He continued on, keeping to the same well-traveled path. Ivkica's grip around his waist became stronger.

"Sing!" she said hoarsely. "Sing Leo Martino!"

Bingula, flustered, began the "Odyssey." Actually, he'd always enjoyed this song. Because of his strong bass voice, he was always asked to sing it at family gatherings, sometimes with guitar accompaniment, which he'd improvise with three chords. He could hardly manage it now, so he switched over to "Bogadi the Secret Agent."

"That one's sad," Ivkica whispered. "Oh, God, we're going to freeze out here."

Bingula filled his lungs with air. Just then, something jumped out in front of them—something white. They both jerked to a halt. Bingula held his breath.

"A rabbit," Ivkica said finally.

"A little rabbit, by God!" Bingula managed.

"A bunny rabbit. He's watching us," Ivkica murmured rapturously. Bingula draped his arm across her shoulders, thinking of how to chase it off.

The white rabbit stopped right in the middle of the path, ten or so feet ahead of them. Then it raised itself up and looked them square in the eye. *Okay,* Bingula thought impatiently. *The rabbit's here, but it'll soon disappear into the forest.* As usual, Bingula had to think ahead. This time he had to think even faster.

Bingula coughed loudly, but the rabbit didn't move. It just cocked one ear to the side. Bingula had a sudden urge to call the Sablics and give them a piece of his mind: first, to keep their noses out of his business, and second, to knock it off with those stories about Ivkica. *Fuck them and their lunches and holiday pastries!* he thought. He had mourned his wife for three years, but it wasn't enough for the Sablics.

A flame had suddenly ignited within him. He wanted to begin a new life now—with Ivkica.

He bent over a bush and broke off an icicle.

"Don't!" Ivkica hissed.

"Don't what?" Bingula waved her away as the rabbit bounced into the night.

"Were you going to throw that at him?" Ivkica asked, pointing to the sharp icicle in his hand.

"Oh, I probably wouldn't have hit him anyway," Bingula said in justification. Ivkica looked relieved and wrapped her arm around his waist once again.

Slowly they made their way through the night, Bingula pleased that he didn't have to deal with her sulking.

He belted out "Don't Think About It, Just Come to Me" with even more gusto than before, as though the decision he'd made about the Sablics a moment ago had given him a second wind.

He continued with "The Sweet Little Snow-Covered Train," then he launched into "The Rooster Song." Finally, out of the blue, he let go with "When I Was a Young Hunter." He sang with all his strength, lungs full of air, stretching out the vowels for all he was worth:

> When I was a young hunter
> Only my mother loved meeeeeeeeeeeeeee.

He sang with emotion, battling against the night, the mountains:

> Rabbit, marten, partriiiiiiiiiidge.

But with every inhalation, every breath, Bingula felt a twinge in his vocal cords. Then immediately, a little lower, he felt a series of sharp pangs, as if a wire were threaded through his capillaries, and it was being yanked tight across his rib cage.

Wild duck and foooooooooox.
Wild duck and foooooooooox.

He squeezed out the tones with surprising clarity, though the
intermittent gusts of wind could have caused distortion.

Bingula loved choral music, especially the sorrowful bass lines
that, like anchors, held the melody within the proper parameters.
For him, his deep voice represented manliness, bravery, and the
ability to keep a situation under control. *And now,* he thought, *now
it's important to maintain the depth of that voice.*

The snow no longer squeaked beneath his feet, and the wind
in the dark arbors of the trees seemed to have lost its strength.
Even the owls were but a dim memory now. Bingula felt his blood
coursing evenly through his body. But he continued to sing—
even though they'd passed the first lanterns, and the snowy path
had changed into a tiled walkway freshly cleared by a snowplow.
He continued to sing, though his songs had long since lost their
purpose: they were no longer needed to dispel the fear.

When he reached the glass doors at the entrance to the lodge,
he pulled the handle with "pull" written above it toward him. They
entered, and the receptionist, alone and holding a receiver in his
hand, gaped at them and the trail of fresh snow they left behind
them on the imitation marble floor.

Ivkica collapsed on a chair in the foyer—a sign to Bingula to end
his song. He kept singing though, out of sheer spite, looking the
receptionist right in the eye:

This is the life of a young hunteeeeeeeeeer.

Then he asked for the key to suite 37. His memory served him
well enough to remember that.

"Where's the dining room?" he asked, conscious of the sharp
pains in his chest.

"I'm sorry, the kitchen closes at 8 PM," the receptionist responded
mechanically, without an iota of sympathy. "That's the daily
schedule," he added, "except Tuesday, when we offer a cold buffet."

The receptionist reminded Bingula of those dried-out types who
were doomed never to reach the age of retirement. As he and Ivkica

climbed the stairs, Bingula was comforted for a moment by the thought of the raw existence mountain-lodge receptionists suffered as a group, but the pain in his thighs prevented him from taking much pleasure in it.

Ivkica, on the other hand, seemed to be in better shape.

Well, after all, she's younger, Bingula thought, allowing her to go ahead of him. When he was her age, he too had a lot more stamina.

He hopped around in the entrance to the apartment, yanking off his boots. It took all his strength to open his suitcase and fumble around until he found his watch.

"It is now ten minutes to eight," he said portentously, as Ivkica walked toward the bathroom with a towel. He heard her turn on the water in the shower, then he heard her bare feet on the tiles.

Still dressed, he lay down with the pillow plumped up under his head. Staring at the ceiling, he tried to recall all the songs he had sung. It occurred to him that he had been incredibly brave. And then, in the space between two faraway refrains, sleep overtook him.

He was awakened by the clattering of a truck beneath his window. The light of a clear mountain morning crept in through an opening in the window shutters. He touched Ivkica's body, which was folded on the other side of the bed.

The first thing he thought of was the Sablics. A phone was on the nightstand, right next to his head. He lifted it onto his chest and dialed their number. As soon as it began to ring, Bingula realized he had no idea what time it was. *Is it too early to be calling?* he worried.

Then he heard Mrs. Sablic's voice: "Sablic residence, may I help you?"

At first, Bingula simply froze. Then he took a deep breath, as though he were preparing for a deep-sea dive, but he was unable to squeeze out a single syllable.

"Hello? Hello?" He heard Mrs. Sablic's voice, the one that reminded him of Sunday mornings, the transistor radio, and soup bubbling on a hot stove.

Sucking in new reserves of air, he gripped the receiver tightly. But all that was left of his powerful bass of the night before was a pitiful, measly "C." The only sound that came out was a whimper.

"Who's there? Hello?" The words echoed in his ear. "Who do you want?"

Just then Bingula felt a warm breath on his chest. Confronted with Ivkica's deep-set eyes looking down at him in the artificial light of the room, he quickly hung up the receiver. He wanted to wish her good morning but remembered just in time that he had lost his voice, and he was overcome with shame.

Battle for Every Last Man

Our young state came into being as a result of indescribable agony, but in the war-torn cities the music scene, though decimated, attempted to maintain continuity under inhuman conditions. In the midst of air raid sirens, artillery attacks, and stray bullets, an additional problem for young rockers was finding practice space. My brother Slaven, who had a band during this miserable period, did something desperate he refuses to discuss to this day. This little story has plagued me for a long time. I wrote five versions, and only with the sixth did I feel I had attained a satisfactory level of condensation. I often read it in public, and it always gives me goosebumps. Maybe that's because of the coldness at the end of the story.

G.N.

the
survival
league

Battle for Every Last Man

Whenever the issue came up, Upchuck would refer to the way things were back then: people packed into the shelters like sardines, hanging wash outside a highly risky proposition, bicycle repair shops flooded with incomprehensible clumps of detritus. In other words, the garage situation was in a state of chaos, and it was impossible to figure out how to get hold of one with electricity. He wasn't trying to justify his behavior now; at any rate, why and to whom? He did it all out of love for the band, which was desperate for a place to practice.

It was no big deal, Upchuck would swear to that. He knew two or three guys who had some juice back then, when the main instruments of persuasion were kitchen knives and razor blades. Pajdo Corak was one of the few people at that time who had a real weapon. And in the dark days of the former regime, both their mothers had the reputation of being loyal "comrades," so Upchuck was fairly sure he would be able to find an old picture of them together in the box of photos on the dresser. No doubt Pajdo had changed a lot since then. The only thing Upchuck heard later about his childhood friend is that he had blown some guy to bits. It was an ethnic thing, was what they said. He did his four-year bit, and when everyone had basically written him off, around the time of the democratic changes in the country, he came back more dangerous than ever, tattooed and glowering.

The first time they ran into each other, Pajdo told him he ought to get a haircut.

"Dangerous times are coming, and everyone's going to have to declare himself!"

But Pajdo's words hadn't really penetrated to Upchuck then. All he had on his mind was the problem of finding some decent basement where the band could practice without being interrupted by a hail of grenades. Upchuck hadn't picked up his Yamaha drums from some garbage dump. He had slaved for years in the tobacco fields for them, his fingers black and sticky, suffering various rashes, itching, insect bites, and even sunstroke. He'd even put his girlfriend on the back burner; it seemed like all she did was suck out his energy. He knew that only by preserving himself and being disciplined could he succeed in getting those drums.

At the last Youth concert he had managed to "appropriate" a cymbal. And then he inherited a bass pedal from a friend who conveniently died. Upchuck lit a candle in his memory every year on the anniversary of his death, said a few rosaries, and changed the water in the vase with the plastic gladiolus. It was the least one could do for a friend, God rest his soul.

They pulled a band together and were tantalizingly close to being able to tape their first demo. All they lacked were the last finishing touches. They knew this, but just at that moment, they were forced to evacuate their little dive because, like all other state-owned properties, it was transformed into a bomb shelter for the blanket brigades.

Now there were bags of rotting groceries hanging from their speakers. It was enough to break your heart. Babies were bawling, and the atmosphere was, shall we say, less than amenable to the heavy metal crowd. And when Pajdo Corak's boys took over the café where Upchuck and his crowd hung out, it was Pajdo, Upchuck had pointed out, who intervened and made sure not a single hair on his head was harmed.

Pajdo also whispered in his ear: "Janja only charges 30 kuna for a haircut. Don't be an idiot." It was then that he got the brainstorm about Pajdo finding them a practice space. Just afternoons, from five to seven. He pulled his hair back into a ponytail and promised to keep the bass down to a minimum and go easy on the cymbals during changeovers. The neighbors had nothing to worry about.

Pajdo Corak came back quickly with an answer. Okay, he said, except one of the band members had to join the Youth section of the ruling party.

"It's purely a formality," he reassured Upchuck, "just a signature on the membership form, and the party will sign over the space. It may be party property, but the acoustics will be great," Pajdo said convincingly.

The band members drew straws. Upchuck got the short end; thus he joined the party. When a registered letter arrived at his home address announcing a party convention, Upchuck's father seethed with fury. "My son! Imagine!" He raged throughout the house while Upchuck considered whether it would do any good to explain his motives. Not a chance, he concluded, so he collected his Yamaha drums and disappeared from home for several days.

The political parties were battling for every last man, so they spent a great deal of energy on accoutrements such as badges, labels, keychains, and plasticized membership cards bearing one's personal photo. These could all be obtained in the local party offices, 24 hours a day. Upchuck gradually eased into the activities of the party's Youth contingent. He never missed a meeting, becoming especially animated when the category "miscellaneous" came up for discussion.

Upchuck knew instinctively that it was not good for a band to take long pauses. So he rejected the "waiting game" tactic, deeming it stupid and unproductive, and simply plunged into the debate. Using the right political jargon—"crisis," "current point in time," "moratorium," and so on—he presented the situation in which the band found itself. He concluded by proposing that the issue of practice space be immediately resolved. It appeared that the members had empathy for the band. The secretary of the regional chapter ushered Upchuck through the room, down the narrow hallway of the renovated barracks, and directly into the head secretary's office.

Upchuck was surprised at the heights to which the position of simple secretary had climbed. In keeping with current fashion, pencil-thin goatees, like toothpicks, held the faces of the party secretaries together, preventing them from collapsing into the center. Goatees, then, were considered crucial to the organization of the country's defenses.

The little room was crammed with additional brochures and materials, and a well-tended fire crackled in the gas stove, visible through the stove's little window. The head secretary gave the impression of a man who was longing to get out of the office and back into the field.

"Yes, of course, yes." He nodded his head as his subordinate explained the problem. Then, scratching his beard, he posed a general question:

"Why are we doing all this?"

"For the future," answered the well-primed subordinate goatee, which though just an iota thinner, was no less defined than that of the head secretary. The subordinate corrected himself immediately: "For what MUST come, Mr. Head Secretary!"

Steam issued from the head secretary's goatee.

"The point of order entitled 'miscellaneous,'" he warned, "provides an opportunity to discuss certain misinterpretations which necessarily arise within convoluted systems of governance. To dissect those issues which at first do not appear to have any connection to direct defense. To, as it were, take instruction from the consummate teachers."

In conclusion, he raised his eyebrows authoritatively. "And our consummate teacher, local secretary, is…?"

"History, head secretary," the thin goatee replied, nodding slightly.

The head secretary smugly yanked a gray hair from the thicket on his head and said, "In our party, we like to refer to the historical example of Laika."*

Upchuck nodded as though this were self-evident.

"Laika was just a young pup when he was forced to assume the responsibility of flying into space; in all the eligibility examinations, he was incomparably superior to the others!" the head secretary reminded them. "A pup!" He approached the window, the gray hair between his fingers, to inspect it in a better light.

"Experience? Form? Habit? Pavlovian reflex?" He counted off the possibilities, as if reciting a questionnaire.

"Bah, contemptible demagogy!" he said with loathing, affirming, for the umpteenth time now, the prejudices that had been inherited from the past.

He let the gray hair do a free fall to the ground then took a firm grip of his military belt and cinched it more tightly. He straightened his legs, adjusted his holster to a reasonable height, and fixed his gaze on the almost deserted parking lot beyond the window. At that moment, the head secretary was in the thrall of a deep and insane belief in a future that would replace the four-wheeled tin cans in the parking lot with German-produced automobiles, all loaded with "state of the art."

"Underground garages are the future," Upchuck blurted out, just like that.

A drop of bad oil crackled in the stove, and for a moment its little window became sooty. The head secretary's eyes swiveled meaningfully toward the subordinate secretary.

"Allot the funds!"

The party memorandum was fed into the electric typewriter.

"Name of the orchestra?" He circled the room, hands clasped at his back.

"Paramilitary Aphids," said Upchuck, stuttering unexpectedly.

"Cross out 'para,' enter 'military,'" said the head secretary.

"Hyphen. Go on: status?"

"Amateur," Upchuck stammered.

"Hyphen, two dots, capital letters. Number of band members who belong to the party Youth section?"

"One," he said, as though in justification.

"Period. Sign here. Thank you."

The head secretary gave Upchuck a firm handshake.

"Young man," he said, turning to him ceremoniously, "we'll be in touch as soon as we listen to your material."

They shook hands. The head secretary had other obligations. He excused himself, saying that defense duties called.

In expectation of a positive resolution, Upchuck stoically endured his father's censure whenever the mailman delivered a party bulletin. He knew why he was putting up with all this, and he was convinced he would be rewarded in the end. However, when Pajdo Corak waltzed into the party office one workday afternoon and, without the slightest hesitation, draped his right arm over Upchuck's left shoulder, he was concerned for the first time over the fate of the band.

It seemed that Pajdo's scars had multiplied in the meantime.

"To make a long story short," Pajdo said, "forget about the practice space." Then he massaged Upchuck's shoulder in a comradely fashion. "The party mistakenly thought you were accordionists."

Pajdo went so far as to apologize: "Sorry, we messed up!"

He said he was going to Bosnia and didn't know when he'd be back. The AK47 hung against his thigh. As he left, he managed to remind Upchuck about the haircut.

"Janja still charges only 30 kuna," he said in recommendation.

Upchuck went along with him. "Right, Pajdo," he said absently, thinking how bad it now looked for the band.

As time went on, Upchuck had the impression that the party apparat was weakening. There were fewer and fewer bulletins, and it seemed as though they had decided to rely only on the pre-war T-shirts and badges with obsolete slogans. Mail from the party decreased, as did invitations to various meetings and conferences. Then one winter day, at a local chapter meeting, the decision was made to reduce the amount of free juice made available to party members. People filed out afterward complaining that it was always the little man who had to suffer.

Night fell earlier and earlier. Then, as Upchuck was shoveling snow around the house, Pajdo, whom he barely recognized, showed up down the street carrying a big notebook under his arm.

The snow squeaked beneath his tennis shoes as he went from house to house, ringing doorbells. It was obvious that he was in a hurry and wanted to finish the party membership revisions as soon as possible, which meant before it got dark. He didn't even enter the yard. Instead, he yelled to Upchuck over the fence, in a voice that indicated a certain intimacy between longtime fellow party members.

"You're still with us, of course, right?"

Upchuck nodded automatically, without taking a moment to think about it. The light was waning, and Pajdo Corak was forced to crane his neck over the fence, as though he were squinting through the snow. The pages of a hardbound notebook gaped open in front of him.

"So, should I put you down for the next quarter?" he repeated impatiently, pressing down on the tip of his ballpoint pen. Like all lefthanders, he held it at too sharp an angle in relation to the paper.

"Write me in, write me in," Upchuck told Pajdo, who wanted a quick answer, perhaps because it was getting dark so fast. Pajdo pressed the pen against the paper, once, twice, three times; it wouldn't write. Upchuck listened to him curse the stupid pen for a few moments then offered him his.

Pajdo took it, wrote, and then, with one practiced movement, fastened the clasp and closed the notebook. His frozen hand pressed the pen into Upchuck's palm, then he stomped off in his tennis shoes through the fresh snow. Darkness engulfed the neighborhood, which was encased in ice. Upchuck opened his fist and realized he was holding a now outdated pen carrying the Youth chapter logo. He began to call out to Pajdo. He held up the pen, unscrewed it between his fingers, then thought to himself: *What would I tell him? To give me back my pen?*

He had a good laugh at his own expense and went into the house. He was glad he hadn't ended up with an ulcer.

Acknowledgments

Ooligan Press is a general trade publisher rooted in the rich literary tradition of the Pacific Northwest. A region widely recognized for its unique and innovative sensibilities, this small corner of America is one of the most diverse in the United States, comprising urban centers, small towns, and wilderness areas. Its residents range from ranchers, loggers, and small business owners to scientists, inventors, and corporate executives. From this wealth of culture, Ooligan Press aspires to discover works that reflect the values and attitudes that inspire so many to call the Northwest their home.

Founded in 2001, Ooligan is a teaching press dedicated to the art and craft of publishing. Affiliated with Portland State University, the press is staffed by students pursuing master's degrees in an apprenticeship program under the guidance of a core faculty of publishing professionals.

The following Portland State University students helped to edit, design, and market *The Survival League*.

✚   **Project Management** - Beth Dillon
Cover Design - Alan Dubinsky
Interior Design - Linda Meyer
Senior Editors - Beth Dillon, Linda Meyer
Editing - Dave Cowsert, Vinnie Kinsella
Proofreading - Laura Daye, Meredith Norwich
Fundraising - Olivia Koivisto, Meredith Norwich
Marketing - Beth Dillon, Sonja Carey, Alan Dubinsky, Jay Evans, Olivia Koivisto, Meredith Norwich

✚ Others involved with *The Survival League*

Bernadette Baker
Bran Bond
Jon Chick
Sean Conners
Laura Dewing
Richard Geller
James Gill
John Graeter
Heather Guidero
Sharon Helms
Kim Hildenbrand
Janice Hussein
Deborah Jayne
Kathryn Juergens
Matt Kelly
Pat Kusch
Melissa Khan
Brynn Kibert
Stefan Lombard
Steve Mayhew
Ali McCart
Adreanne Mispelon
Mary Putnam
Anabel Ramirez
Leslie Royal
Connie Spiegel
Summer Steele
Viviana Tornero
Kevin Vandehey
Jennifer Whipple
Nan Wilder
Lamont Wilkins

About the Author

Gordan Nuhanović was born in 1968 in Vinkovci, Croatia. He worked as a war reporter during the Homeland War and is presently a journalist and literary critic in Croatia. He is the literary commentator for the main weekly television program in Zagreb devoted to book reviews and literary topics. His short stories have appeared in numerous literary journals, and his short story collections in Croatian include *Liga za Opstanak* (*The Survival League*), 2002, and *Bitka Za Svakog Čovjeka* (*Battle for Every Last Man*), 2003. He received the Society of Croatian Writers' Nightingale Award and the Ivan and Josip Kozarac Award for *Liga za Opstanak*, and the Croatian daily newspaper *Jutarnji List* voted this collection one of the top five books published in 2002.

Nuhanović was lead vocalist in one of Croatia's leading punk rock bands, Short Circuit. In 1989 he founded the "Young Croatians' Iggy Pop Preservation Group," whose purpose was to preserve the popularity of Iggy Pop and attend all his concerts. He continues to serve as the group's honorary president.

Printed in the USA
CPSIA information can be obtained
at www.ICGtesting.com
JSHW012040140824
68134JS00033B/3172

9 781932 010060